Other Books by Kandi Jaynes

August in Montana
A Widow's Scars

A Dream to be Loved

A Dream to be Loved

By

Kandi Jaynes

Desert Breeze Publishing, Inc.
27305 W. Live Oak Rd #424
Castaic, CA 91384

http://www.DesertBreezePublishing.com

Copyright © 2012 by Kandi Jaynes
ISBN 10: 1-61252-839-2
ISBN 13: 978-1-61252-839-7

Published in the United States of America
Electronic Publish Date: May 2012
Print Publish Date: October 2013

Editor-In-Chief: Gail R. Delaney
Content Editor: Theresa Stillwagon
Marketing Director: Jenifer Ranieri
Cover Artist: Gwen Phifer

Cover Art Copyright by Desert Breeze Publishing, Inc © 2012

All rights reserved. No portion of this book may be reproduced or transmitted in any form or by any electronic or mechanical means, including photocopying, recording or by any information retrieval and storage system without permission of the publisher.

Names, characters and incidents depicted in this book are products of the author's imagination, or are used in a fictitious situation. Any resemblances to actual events, locations, organizations, incidents or persons – living or dead – are coincidental and beyond the intent of the author.

Dedication

To my family and friends who have all been so incredibly supportive of my writing endeavors. I am so very blessed to have such a wonderful support system.

Chapter One

"Drake, I'm so glad you're finally joining our team." Bill Denison slapped him on the back as he walked by on the way to his chair. "I always knew you'd be a great asset to the company, but I must admit, I was beginning to lose hope it would ever happen. I won't dwell on that though, you're here now, and that's what counts."

"I've looked over the reports you gave me," Drake stated. "I'm impressed. You have a knack for predicting the market."

"I've made my mistakes, but all in all, I've been pretty lucky. I'm not afraid to take chances on new products. Most of the other companies have been in business long enough they rely on variations of the old standbys. I just don't happen to believe that is where the future is." He picked up a cigar, twirling it between his fingers. With a twinkle in his eye, he said, "So as the new Vice President over manufacturing, I expect you to remember that."

Drake straightened his long legs, crossing his ankles. "I'll try to keep that in mind," he said with a grin, then added more seriously, "I'll need to get the lay of the land. See how production is managed and the general flow of inventory start to finish. I'd like to meet with some of the supervisors to get their input."

"I agree, all that is important. You aren't scheduled to start until next week, however, so I've arranged for some sample cases to be put together for you. Take them home and familiarize yourself with the new product lines. That way, when you do get out in the shop, you can concentrate on how things are being produced instead of what is being produced. It might save you some time. Some of our new pieces are quite different from what you saw here years ago."

"Thanks, that'll be helpful."

"Actually, many things are quite different than they were the last time you were here. Two years ago we expanded, nearly doubling the size of the building. We built all new offices, tearing out all the old ones to expand the shop. We added a new state of the art clean and sterile area, a much larger, more efficient shipping and receiving department, and a break room finally big enough to accommodate everybody. We've added on so many new people it's hard for me to keep up with them all. I know you're trying to get moved. You can wait and take the official tour later." Bill glance longingly at the unlit cigar. "So, how are you settling in?"

"Fine I guess. I don't much care for apartment living, but I have to stay somewhere until I can find someplace permanent."

"If you had a wife she could help you in that department. Any prospects?"

"Not one," replied Drake, letting out a loud slow breath.

"Surely you don't have any trouble getting dates. You're a young, intelligent, good-looking guy. You make a good living. So what's the problem? Don't you want to get married?"

"Actually, I would like to find a wife and start a family. The problem is finding Miss Right." He leaned his head on the back of the chair, staring blankly at the ceiling tiles. "The job I had in Indianapolis was very demanding. I didn't have a lot of time for socializing. The only women I really saw were the ones I met through work. That usually turned out one of two ways. Some were the professional career woman type. Intelligent and ambitious, but often tried to turn our relationship into a competition, wanting to prove they could do their job every bit as good as a man. Instead of wanting to relax or get to know each other when we were out, they spent the evening wanting to compare daily accomplishments." He stretched and yawned.

"Then there were the women who weren't worried about having a career. They were more than willing to get to know me and spend the evening doing whatever I wanted to do, as long as my bank account came along. Some would have loved to be the docile housewife and live in a penthouse with a closet full of designer clothes and expensive jewelry." He raised his head and looked at Bill. "Don't get me wrong, if I were to marry, I'd never begrudge my wife anything I own. I just don't want what I own to be the reason she marries me."

Bill tapped his cigar on the ashtray, "So what are you looking for in a wife?"

Drake grinned. "Just the usual. Someone who's intelligent, funny, gorgeous, and adores my every quality."

The older man laughed. "Well, it's nice to know you haven't set your sights too high."

"I want someone somewhere between high powered career woman and expensive pushover. Someone versatile enough to enjoy a big city now and then, but doesn't need an expensive high society life to be happy. Kind and loving on one hand," one side of his mouth curled upward and an eyebrow lifted slightly, "But with just enough of a feisty streak to keep it interesting."

Bill chuckled. "I hope you find her. She sounds great."

Drake pinched the bridge of his nose, surprised at himself for talking so openly about this subject, but too tired to care. "I've about given up. Why does it have to be so hard? I just want to look at a woman and know she's the right one. I'm tired of wasting time dating someone only to find out she's not right for me. Wouldn't it be great if Miss Right would just walk up and announce herself somehow? Something like, 'Hi, nice to meet you. I'm just a hometown girl who wants to enjoy life to the fullest'. It would be nice to meet a girl who isn't too uptight to order dessert once in awhile. Someone who, when asked what their favorite restaurant is, names some quiet out of the way place where you can just go and be yourself instead of a stuffy pompous overpriced one, because it's the most prestigious place to be."

Bill laughed again. "You have always managed to get what you want out of life, but I think having Miss Right come up and casually announce herself is asking a bit much, even for you. I know you're discouraged, but give it time. You're only thirty-five, you have plenty of time. Maybe once you get settled in here you can start looking for that hometown girl." Bill glanced again at his unlit cigar. "Maybe your Miss Right won't make you give up your simple pleasures in life." He grumbled good-naturedly before setting the cigar back on the ashtray. "You look exhausted. You should go home and get some rest."

"I haven't had much sleep the last few days. Between packing and trying to tie up loose ends at my old job, I've been working around the clock."

"You get some rest and tomorrow I'll have the product information sent over to you. Then you'll have the rest of the week to look it over. This weekend, Marcia wants to have you over for dinner. She'll call you with the details."

Drake stood up and shook Bill's hand. "Thanks, that sounds like a good plan. See you this weekend then. Tell Marcia I'm looking forward to it."

*****

Kate started every Monday morning the same. She would sit down with a tooling report and decide what needed to be ordered. She'd been doing this for the last two years. That was when the company had expanded yet again and the tooling and raw materials had been split into separate departments. She had been transferred to day shift and put in charge of the tool crib. It was now located at one end of the machine shop and enclosed behind an eight-foot high chain link fence. A window had been cut out of the fence with a steel platform fastened across the bottom of the open square like a small table. This was where tools and fixtures were handed in and out. Immediately to the left of the window, was a desk with a computer and to the right, a small door set on rails that slid open and shut. Large metal shelves against one sidewall and across the back were filled with miscellaneous supplies. Another small door had been put in the back corner. The other wall to just left of the computer desk contained five large cabinets with drawers holding most of the cutting tools and a small desk where Kate usually did paperwork. Many rows of shelves lined the middle of the area housing all the machine fixtures. Some still called it the tool crib, but most now just referred to it as the cage.

A bell had been hooked up beside the window so when someone needed something they could get the attendant's attention. Kate was busy with her report when she heard the bell. Putting the pages down, she headed for the window.

"Hi, Kate, I need a new drill bit. This one is shot."

"Hi, Dave, quarter inch, isn't it? I just put some away."

"Great. Hey what have you heard about the new VP?"

Kate grinned, "What makes you think I've heard anything?"

Dave laughed. "You hear everything around here. With the exception of a few office workers, everyone in the building has to come to you for supplies. You hear news from every department. So what's the scoop?"

"All I know is he starts today. I heard he's a friend of Mr. Denison."

"That's all anybody seems to know. Word is he's probably some old stodgy guy who's set in his ways. I hope he doesn't turn out to be some drill sergeant type."

"I don't think Mr. Denison would hire someone like that, do you?"

"No, probably not. Denison is a pretty nice guy. Do you know the new guy's name?"

Kate cocked her head, "Let me think. I don't remember for sure, Mallard? Mandarin? It seems like it had something to do with a duck."

"A duck?"

"I don't remember, but we'll probably find out today."

Ten minutes later, Kate was finishing up her orders when she heard a thump at the window. She looked up to see Smitty walking away. Getting out of her chair she marched in his direction. "Berkley!"

With her hands on her hips, she didn't so much as flinch as the angered man more than twice her size approached. Smitty glared down at her. "How many times have I told you not to call me that?" He ground out between clenched teeth.

Not daunted in the least, she replied, "The exact same number of times I've told you I'm not your mother or your maid. You know better than to bring me something like this." She pointed at the fixture he had just returned. It was dripping with cutting oil and covered with razor sharp steel shavings. "I don't hand things out looking like that, do I? I expect it to be returned looking like it did when you got it. Take it back, and don't return it until it's clean."

Smitty's shoulders dropped, as much as it was possible for them to drop anyway, and he let out a sigh. Picking up the fixture, he looked at her and conceded, "I'll clean it up." Holding the piece of steel in one hand, he pulled a shop rag out of his back pocket with the other and wiped up the oil that had dripped onto the table. Then he turned and strode to his machine.

Kate grinned as she watched his retreat. She and Smitty had started in the shop within a week of each other and had become instant friends. They both lived alone and helped each other out from time to time. Kate would occasionally cook a meal for him and he would help her fix things around the house when it was more than she could handle. She was probably closer to him than anyone else in the shop. She thought of him as an adopted brother.

Kate stepped from the window and turned to find two men staring at her. One of the men she recognized immediately. The other man she had never seen before. That face, with its dark tan, high prominent cheekbones and chiseled chin, was not one she would have forgotten. He stood just over six-feet she guessed, with sun bleached streaks running through his brown hair and incredible blue eyes. Maybe they were actually gray; she couldn't tell for sure this far away. He had very long legs and a tapered waist. The snug polo shirt he wore outlined a nicely sculpted chest and broad shoulders.

"Hi, Kate," Bill said as he approached her.

She shook herself mentally. Over the years she had worked with more men than she could count, but couldn't remember ever absorbing every detail of one instantly like she had just done with this one. She smiled at Bill and returned his greeting, trying to concentrate on him and not the man beside him.

"I knew you were no slouch when it came to dealing with the men out there, but I'm not sure I would have the nerve to talk to Smitty like that."

Kate laughed. "He's big, but he's really very nice. He would stand down a grizzly bear without blinking, but would never think of hurting a woman. Which is lucky for me considering how often I irritate him."

"What was it you called him? Berkley?"

Kate turned and looked behind her. "I wouldn't let him hear you say that. I wouldn't have said it if I'd known anybody was listening." She glanced toward the shop again then grinned. "Believe it or not his real name is Berkley Worthington Smithers, the third," she said in her snootiest voice.

"You're kidding?"

"No, I'm not. He would probably make an exception to his no-hurting-women rule if he knew I told you though, so I'd appreciate it if you wouldn't let on you know."

"That secret is safe with us. Isn't that right, Drake?"

"Right."

Kate felt, as much as heard, his deep baritone reply.

"Kate, this is Drake Hampton, the new Vice President of Manufacturing. I'm giving him a tour. Drake, this is Kate Layton. If there is anything you need to get a job done, Kate's the one to see."

Drake held out his hand. "Hello."

"Hello, it's nice to meet you." She stifled a nervous giggle as she slipped her hand into his. They only shook hands briefly, but it sent a strange tingle up her arm.

"Is something funny?"

"Um, lets just say from the rumors I've heard, you're not quite what I was expecting."

"Let me guess," said Bill, "Everyone was expecting some old crony I was saving from retirement."

Kate laughed. "Something like that, yes."

"Drake here is a friend of mine. I met him through my son when they were roommates in college. I've been trying to get him to join the team for years. He's been working in Indianapolis for the past five years."

"Really? Indy is great."

"You like the city?" Drake asked.

"My friends and I occasionally drive down to spend the weekend. We always have a great time. I like to visit, but I don't think I'd want to live there. Basically, I'm just a hometown girl. The city seems so busy. Here, I feel like I have time to enjoy life."

The way Drake stared at her made her very uneasy. Not to mention the fact that Bill suddenly glanced from her to Drake with the oddest grin. She tried not to fidget under the scrutiny.

Kate looked nervously at them both. She wiped the tip of her nose with the rag in her hand. "Do I have a smudge on my nose or something? I quite often get oil or coolant on my face."

"No my dear, you're lovely as ever." Bill glanced again from her to Drake.

She turned, trying to hide the blush she felt spread through her cheeks at the compliment.

Bill spoke again, his voice tinged with amusement. "Kate, Drake has been busy moving and hasn't had time to learn the area yet. Maybe you could recommend a place to eat. What is your favorite restaurant?"

"Well my personal favorite is the Mocha and Mousse coffee house."

Bill's brow creased. "Where's that?"

"It's on the ground floor of an old brick building over in Pierceton. With a concrete floor and painted cinder block walls it's not a fancy place, but they have great food if you like soups and sandwiches. They make all their own bread and croissants. They, of course, have all manner of coffees and sodas. The best part is there's a pastry chef on staff. The desserts they serve are incredible." Then she grinned. "I have to admit, I don't often see many executives there."

Bill turned to Drake and clapped his shoulder laughing. "That just about covers the list, doesn't it?"

Drake never took his eyes off Kate, but he did smile. "Yes, it sure does."

Kate was thoroughly confused. "What list?"

Just then Mr. Denison was paged. He stepped to the phone at Kate's desk and received a quick message. "Well Drake, that conference call we've been expecting just came in. We'd better go."

Drake stepped in front of Kate and took her hand. He didn't shake it as she thought he was going to, he just held it in one hand and covered the back of it with his other. She wanted to pull away, but couldn't seem to move as his gaze penetrated hers. Gray, thought Kate. His eyes are definitely gray.

Then Drake ever so softly said, "It is so nice to meet you, Kate."

Bill chuckled behind him and he released her hand.

Kate noticed the knowing look the two men exchanged. "Am I missing something here?"

Bill laughed again. "I suspect you'll figure it out soon enough." The two men left through the door they had entered, leaving Kate to stare after them with lines of worry creasing her brow.

*****

Drake hadn't wanted to leave the tool crib. Something about that woman had him completely captivated. He couldn't keep the word feisty out of his mind after what he had just witnessed.

He was amazed at the sheer size of the man she had yelled at. The guy stood at least six foot six and was built like a pro wrestler. The black leather vest covering his white T-shirt stretched tight across his massive chest. As he returned to the window a tattoo of the grim reaper became visible on his right bicep, which was the diameter of an average man's thigh.

She stood with her back to him undaunted by the hulk of a man staring her down. A braid of chestnut hair started at the base of her smooth slim neck, continued past the petite squared shoulders to the middle of her perfectly contoured back. His gaze had fallen from there to appreciate the nicely rounded hips just above those long slender legs. He hadn't been able to take his eyes off her.

When she finally turned around, she had taken his breath away. Kate had incredible brown eyes, sharp and intelligent.

Drake was brought out of his musing when Bill spoke.

"Well, I guess I was wrong when I said you were asking too much. She's a terrific girl. I've always had a very high opinion of her. I realize this coincidence doesn't mean the two of you will end up together, but when I think about it, the two of you might hit it off quite nicely."

"Bill," came Drake's self-assured reply. "We're going to do more than simply hit it off. That," he nodded his head toward the cage, "is the girl I'm going to marry."

Chapter Two

An hour later, Kate saw the two men out on the shop floor, obviously continuing their tour. She tried to concentrate on her work, but found herself watching Drake instead. Disgusted with herself, she decided to check inventory in the back so she couldn't see him. After counting the same stack of polishing buffs three times, however, and still not being sure how many there were, she gave up. She slammed one of the buffs down, grating, "What is wrong with you?" out loud.

"That buff giving you trouble, is it?" She spun to find Ray, her supervisor, standing behind her.

She grimaced, "No. I'm just having a bad day."

"I hope you're not worried about the new VP. I've talked to him he seems like a pretty good guy. I know everyone's been tense about someone new taking over, but I think the transition will go pretty smoothly."

"I'm not worried about that, really." She wasn't worried about Drake doing his job. She was worried about her job if she couldn't find a way to concentrate with him in the building.

"Have you had a chance to meet him yet?"

"Yes. Mr. Denison brought him through here this morning."

"What did you think of him?"

"I, ah...well, guess he seemed... nice," she stammered. "I only really talked to him a minute or two before they were called away."

"Are you okay? I don't think I've ever seen you this rattled before."

She gave the most reassuring smile she could muster, "I'm fine really. It's just been a difficult day. You know how Monday's can be."

"Yes, I do," he laughed, "Which is the reason I'm here." He held up a tool. One end of it resembled a melted candle made of black wax with an occasional hint of blue.

"Looks like someone ran it backwards."

"Yep. I took my eyes off one of the trainees for a few minutes. At least it happened after Denison and the new guy had moved on."

She laughed in agreement. "That probably wouldn't have made a good first impression."

Kate kept herself busy the rest of the day, but didn't feel like she had really accomplished anything. She was relieved when it was time to clock out.. That thought disturbed her. She had always loved her job and although there were times she was glad to leave because of being tired or having plans after work, she didn't remember ever just wanting to get out of the building.

On the drive home her thoughts took her back to when she had started five years earlier.

*****

She had been thrilled when she had landed the job as janitor. Not that she liked cleaning, but it was a job that got her in the door of a company growing fast enough she knew there was potential to move into a full time position with better pay and benefits.

She grimaced as she remembered her first day. The man who hired her had failed to tell her, working the evening shift, she would be the only woman in the building. Not that it would have kept her from taking the job, it just would have been nice to be warned. She was used to being around people of the male persuasion, having grown up around so many. It just gave her an uneasy feeling to work in the dark, quiet areas alone, in a building containing so many men she didn't know.

That's how she met Mr. Denison. She had been deep in thought with the drone of the vacuum cleaner surrounding her when someone tapped her on the shoulder. She jumped, and let out a scream she was sure echoed in every corner of the building. She turned to find a man grasping his chest and trying to catch his breath.

Kate grabbed his arm. "I'm so sorry, are you all right?"

"I will be. I didn't intend to startle you young lady." It suddenly dawned on Kate who the man was and she let go of his arm. She had seen his picture in the lobby. He was the president and CEO of the company. Her heart sank. She had just nearly killed the man who ran the entire business. So much for her new job.

As it turned out, he had just wanted to let her know he was leaving for the day and apologized for any inconvenience his random hours cause her. Which impressed her greatly. She felt even better about her job knowing she worked in a place where the man in charge took the time to, not only know, but be polite to all his employees.

She had met most of the men who worked her shift the second night while she cleaned the break room. They all came in, introduced themselves and chatted with her while she worked.

Although she wasn't bad with most domestic activities, and was actually a good cook, she had always been very mechanically inclined. She loved working with her hands and understood tools and machinery better than most other things. She could fix most things around the house when needed. Not that there was much to fix in the small two room apartment she lived in.

That would change though. She was on her way to owning a house of her own. It wouldn't be a huge house, or one with lots of fancy extras, but it would be hers. All hers. No more being tossed from family member to family member. Nobody would be able to ask her to leave, because they were either tired of her, or needed the room for someone more important. So far she had worked hard and kept on schedule with her plans. Step one: get a full time job after high school. Step two: move into an apartment by age nineteen. Step three: a place by herself by age twenty-two. Step four: Homeowner by age twenty-six.

She was on step three now. Only one more to go, and three years to do it. *Someday,* she dreamed, *a place of my own, just for me.*

Her friends, Missy, Kelsie, and Sue continuously asked her about all the men she worked with and what they were like and how many of them were single.

"I can't believe you're the one who works in a building with all men," grumbled Sue. "Why can't it be one of us who would be more than willing to take advantage of the situation?"

"Because none of you would be willing to clean toilets or mop floors for a living."

"Okay, I'll give you that, but how can you resist all that testosterone? All those tight jeans and bulging biceps?"

"So far it's not been a problem. I have my sights set higher than mere men. I want a..."

"We know, we know, a house of your own, and no one to answer to." The three said in unison.

Kate smiled innocently. "Oh, have I mentioned that before?"

"Only for as long as we've known you," Kelsie answered. The four of them had become friends in the ninth grade and had been close ever since.

They all glared at her, and she sighed. "Tell you what, after our traditional Saturday night pizza and gab session why don't we head down to Pete's for a game of pool? I might happen to know some of the guys hanging out there."

"Now you're talking. You know, you just might turn out to be a useful member of this group after all," Sue quipped.

"Thanks," Kate answered sarcastically.

As they entered Pete's she noticed some of the men from work. "Hey, you finally decided to come." One of them yelled from across the room.

"Finally?" Sue murmured.

"Well, actually they have asked me to join them the last few weeks."

Sue reached up and pinched the back of Kate's arm.

"Ouch! What was that for?"

"Jut because you don't like men doesn't mean the rest of us don't. You could have brought us here weeks ago and didn't."

"I like men," Kate replied indignantly. "I just don't feel the need to throw myself at them." She didn't mention that since she had hired on full-time in the shop she had been asked out occasionally. After politely declining enough invitations with the excuse of not wanting to get involved with someone she worked with, word got around and she had stopped being asked.

Sue waved her hand in the air. "Yeah, yeah, whatever. Now introduce us to them. Ooh, all of them," she said as they made their way across the room.

Kate sat and watched as her friends flirted, smiled, and giggled. It really was a sight to behold. Sue, the most outgoing of them all, had no trouble keeping the conversation flowing.

Men were always attracted to her. She had silky black hair that bounced and waved around her heart-shaped face. Combined with her large green eyes, long dark lashes, and supermodel figure, which was always wrapped in attire flashy enough to match her personality, it wasn't hard to see why Sue never lacked for company.

Kate supposed that was good because Sue had a short attention span where men were concerned. She liked variety and never stayed with any one man too long.

Sitting beside Sue was Kelsie. She always went along in whatever adventurous scheme was decided on for fun, but was usually more of an observer than a participant. With her dark hair and dark eyes that shone out of the smooth pale skin covering her delicate features, she was the quiet, shy one of the group.

Missy was next. She was the dramatic one. Always pointing out the possible consequences of everyone's actions, good and bad. She could come up with more reasons why someone should or should not do something than anyone Kate had ever known. She never left the house unless her blond hair had been curled and styled perfectly. Always immaculately dressed in colors she felt best complimented her, she believed one should always be at their best when out in public because you never know who you might run into.

Kate looked down at herself. She was known as the easygoing one, always willing to just go with the flow. Very little ever upset or rattled her. She wasn't as pretty as her friends. She usually wore jeans and tee shirts. She did own a dress, but couldn't remember the last time she had actually worn it. She considered herself to have an average figure. Except for the short cropping of bangs sweeping across her forehead, her plain brown hair was always kept in a braid down the middle of her back. It was just easier that way. It kept it out of her face and didn't have to be styled everyday.

Her friends were obviously enjoying the attention they were receiving from her coworkers. She was somewhat surprised how much she was also enjoying the evening. Some of the men had occasionally flirted with her at work, but she knew better than to take it seriously. She had grown up with countless males; her dad, uncles, cousins, and any number of their friends. The house seemed to have a revolving door for anyone who had wanted to live there.

With all those people around, there had not always been room for her. She was always the youngest and, other than her mother, the only girl. She learned early on that, although she could occasionally be considered an amusing diversion, she would never be the most important person in anyone's life.

She didn't relate well to people on a personal level. She talked to her friends and told them many things, but always held part of herself back. A part she couldn't let go. Therefore, she came to accept long ago, marriage was not an option for her. That's not to say she didn't notice when a man was good looking, or occasionally wonder what it would be like to be one of those girls men actually wanted to date, but she accepted that for what it was... idle daydreaming.

Now and then one of her friends would set her up on a date. She would usually go to keep the peace, and most of the time enjoyed the evening, but never went out with anyone more than once. After all, what would be the point? They wouldn't want a long-term relationship, and she knew she wasn't capable of a casual affair.

As the months passed and Kate got to know all the men at work better, she also became more interested in the work being done. She began to spend her breaks out in the shop asking questions about the machines and the tools they used. Over time she had learned about the parts being made as well as the different fixtures used to hold them in the machines, tooling, gauges, and many other aspects of production. Most of the men were more than willing to answer her questions, even seemed to enjoy teaching her about what they did.

When six months had passed, she was called into her supervisor's office. She was offered a full time position dealing with raw materials and tooling that came with substantial pay increase.

*****

Present Day

Kate pulled into her drive, stopped, and just looked at her house. Even after almost two years of being here she still couldn't believe it was hers. She had worked hard to save a large down payment, then just when she started house hunting she transferred to days and her current job. She had gotten another substantial raise.

Kate leaned back in her seat. She had known this was the one the first time she saw the house and its one-acre lot. In the front yard two giant oak trees towered high above the roof providing complete shade from the afternoon sun. The back yard was home to a large silver maple and two decorative redbud trees.

The house was a light blue ranch style with an attached garage, and a fireplace. It had three bedrooms, which was nice considering how often her friends stayed over. It sat on a hill just high enough to give her a fantastic view of woods and rolling wheat fields. The garage was behind. One could follow the drive around back and park, or follow a small U looping around an oak in the front. Depending on where you parked

A Dream to be Loved

you could enter the house through the front door in the living room or the back into the kitchen.

Her nearest neighbor was a half-mile down the road. This was the first place she felt truly at home in many years. She put the car in gear and pulled into the garage, wanting nothing more than to curl up in front of a fire with a cup of tea.

She took a shower and put on her favorite shorts and one of her uncle's old shirts. She smiled as she looked at the frayed garment. It was getting quite tattered. Time for a trip to Max and Ruth's, she thought.

As a kid she would sometimes stay at her aunt and uncle's farm. The first time or two she stayed she had forgotten a nightgown, so her aunt had let her wear one of Max's old button up shirts. Kate liked it so much she asked if she could have it when she left and took it home. From then on she would purposely forget to pack a nightgown. After awhile, when Ruth would clean out closets, she would give Kate all of Max's old shirts. It was a tradition that continued to this day.

Over the next few days she managed to get some work done. She saw Drake occasionally pass through the shop, but luckily he hadn't returned to the cage. He did however smile that weird, knowing smile at her and wave whenever he saw her. It unnerved her, but she did her best to hide it.

On Thursday afternoon she was filling a tool order when the phone rang. She answered it and was surprised to discover Mr. Denison's assistant on the other end. When she hung up Terry was standing at the window watching her. "What's up? Bad news?"

"I don't know. I've just been called on the carpet."

Terry whistled low. "Do you have any idea what for?"

"No, I don't. Viv said Mr. Denison wants to see me in an hour." Kate answered, checking her watch.

"Holy cow! The big guy himself summoned you?"

"Yes. I wish I had some idea why. Have you heard of any major tooling problems?"

"No, I haven't. Hey Jeff." He yelled as he saw another coworker not far away.

"Whatcha need?" Jeff strolled over to the cage.

"Have you heard of any problems involving the tool crib lately?"

"No, nothing why?"

"Mr. Denison wants to see Kate in his office."

"Wow. Well, don't be too worried. The top dog doesn't do the firing. He has other people to do that for him."

"Gee thanks, I feel so much better now," she replied. "Here's your tooling, Terry."

"Thanks, and good luck."

Kate was a nervous wreck for the next hour. She liked Bill and had gotten the impression he liked her. He had always made a point of coming to talk to her whenever he was out in the shop, but had never called her to his office before. The hour finally passed and she wound her way through the maze of hallways to Mr. Denison's office. Viv announced her, then said she was to go right in. Bill stood as she entered and asked her to sit.

"How are you, Kate?"

"I'm fine, sir."

"I'm sorry to disrupt your afternoon like this but I have a rather unusual request." He returned to his seat and leaned toward her. "I know this is short notice but I was wondering if you have any plans for tomorrow evening?"

Kate stared at him for a moment confused. Then slowly said. "No, I don't."

"Good, good. Now I know this is a terrible imposition, but would you be willing to go to a business dinner of sorts?"

Kate looked even more confused. "Business dinner?"

"I know it's somewhat out of the ordinary, but Drake wants to get input from some of the key members of manufacturing. He has already talked to some of the machinists and gotten their thoughts on improving production. Now he wants to get other viewpoints as well. The tool crib plays a large roll in keeping production running smoothly."

"The men out on the line are easy to talk to while they work. Members of management are different. They do troubleshooting all over, and people are constantly making demands on their time. You may stay in the cage, but there is a constant stream of interruptions. This is strictly voluntary of course, but we would appreciate it if you could attend this dinner to give your input and answer any questions that have arisen."

Kate was trying to maintain composer. Dinner with Drake, her stomach flopped just thinking about it. Of course other members of management would be there. It's not like it would be just her and Drake. She took a deep, calming breath. She had to quit over reacting where this man was concerned. He was just a man after all. She owed Mr. Denison a lot. This company had helped her achieve her goals, her dreams. She had a job she loved, and was paid well for doing it. If he wanted this one favor, she would do it. How bad could it be?

She smiled as much as her tense cheeks would allow. "I'd be more than happy to help in anyway I can. As far as I know I can attend the dinner. What time will it be, and where?"

"Great. I'll send a car for you at six thirty."

"Oh, that won't be necessary. I can just meet them there."

"Nonsense. Someone will be by to get you. It will be a casual dinner. I hope you don't mind."

"Of course not. That sounds fine."

"Good. Just leave your address with Viv." He came around the desk and shook her hand patting the back of it while he did so. "Don't look so worried. I'm sure it will be fun."

"Yes sir, I'm sure it will." She smiled and left his office.

By the time she got back to the cage, she only had about twenty minutes before the end of her shift. She had to rush to get everything done and ready for the next shift to come in and take over.

The next day was so busy she didn't have time to fret over the thought of the business dinner. Besides, she had done enough of that the night before. Many mishaps happened that day and fresh tooling was in high demand.

She was tired by the time she pulled into her drive and wanted nothing more than a nice long soak in the tub. As she was entering the house she heard a ruckus in the kitchen, and smiled as familiar voices drifted across the room. "You know, for people who made fun of me for so many years about wanting my own house, you sure spend an awful lot of time here."

"We wouldn't want you to get lonely," Missy replied.

"Besides you have a better kitchen than I do," Sue added. "You look tired. Rough day?"

"Yes, it was."

"That new VP was supposed to start this week, wasn't he? Have you met him yet?"

Kate choked slightly on the tea Missy had handed her. "I, ah... well yes, I did met him." She cleared her throat, "I mean, meet him."

"So what's the old guy like? Do you think he'll want to make a lot of drastic changes?"

"I don't know. I mean, I only talked to him for a few minutes. He seemed, well, I don't know... okay, I suppose. He's just... well, he's new. It's hard to tell yet what he'll want to do." By the time she finished rambling both of her friends stared at her like she had just grown purple horns.

"What is wrong with you?" Sue demanded. "I've never seen you not be able to finish a complete sentence before. Is the old guy that bad? Did he come on to you or something?"

"No!" she screeched, then cleared her throat again and continued. "He didn't come on to me. It was just a strange meeting. I don't know, he almost acted like he knew something about me that even I don't know." She took a sip of tea and tried to change the subject. "Where's Kelsie?"

"She ran to the store to get some soda. You're out. You really should keep up with these things you know."

"Sorry, but it's difficult to keep stocked up when other people come in and help themselves whenever they please." She returned with their usual good natured banter.

"So, tell us about the old coot."

"What old coot?" asked Kelsie as she entered the room loaded down with bottles.

"Kate's new VP," Sue answered.

"He's not mine! I mean, well, there just isn't much to tell."

"There must be something to tell or you wouldn't be so flustered. What is it about the old coot that has you so rattled?"

Kate let out a soft sigh. She knew Sue well enough to know she wouldn't let this go. "First of all he's not old. And he's not a coot."

Sue's eyebrows rose. "Really. Now we're getting somewhere. So how not old and not a coot, is he?"

"He's in his mid thirties. He just moved up here from Indy. He seems to be well liked out in the shop."

"So," Sue grinned and wriggled her eyebrows. "How well liked is he in the tool crib?"

"He seems nice enough."

"What does he look like?" Missy asked.

"Tall. Light brown hair. You know, the usual." Kate looked at her watch. "I have an appointment this evening I have to get ready for. I'm going to go take a bath." She hopped out of her chair and tore down the hall as fast as she could without actually running.

By the time she climbed out of the tub she felt much better. She spent half an hour trying to decide what to wear. Something she had never done before. She finally decided on her newest pair of jeans and an ivory sweater that belonged to Missy. Instead of the standard braid, her hair hung loose down her back. The sides were drawn up into a clip in the back to keep it out of her face. She even put on earrings. "I can't believe I'm doing this," she mumbled as she slipped them on. She checked her watch. It was a quarter after six. She took a deep breath, closed her eyes, and let it out slowly. Looking in the mirror, she said. "You can do this. You work with over a hundred men every day. You can handle one dinner with a small group." She didn't hear anything as she walked down the hall. She had purposely taken extra time to be sure everyone would be gone and she wouldn't have to answer any more questions.

Kelsie and Missy still came over often, but usually didn't stay long when they did. They both had other commitments now. Kelsie had married Tom, a loan officer from a local bank, just over a year ago. She now worked part-time at the library. Missy was a teller at the bank where Tom worked and had recently gotten engaged to John, who ran a small print shop in town. Kate liked both men and was happy for her friends. Sue was the one Kate saw most often. She still enjoyed her work as a travel agent and her commitment free lifestyle.

Kate stopped dead in her tracks when she walked into the kitchen and saw all three of them perched at the table.

Sue whistled. "Wow. Exactly what kind of appointment is this?"

A Dream to be Loved

"It's actually a business dinner. Mr. Denison called me in yesterday and asked if I would attend."

"Isn't that my sweater?" Missy asked.

Kate looked down. "Yes. You've seen my wardrobe. I don't have anything suitable to wear to a business dinner." Then quipped, "Besides, if you don't want me to borrow things don't leave them at my house."

"It looks great on you. Are those earrings?"

"Do we have to make such a big deal about this?"

"Yes, actually we do," Sue answered. "How often do we see you dressed up? Where are you going?"

"I don't know, Mr. Denison didn't tell me."

"How are you supposed to get there?" Missy asked.

"He insisted on sending a car for me. It should be here any minute." Kate walked over and got a drink of water. She didn't know why her mouth was so dry this evening. As she was setting the glass in the sink a car pulled up the drive.

"Wow," Sue said. "That's a nice car."

When the doorbell rang they all followed her into the living room. Kate pulled the door open and stood there in shock.

"Hello, Kate," rumbled a deep sexy voice.

"I... hello Mr. Hampton." Her purse slipped from her hand, hitting the floor with a thud, and she stooped to retrieve it. As she straightened, Sue stepped over and casually guided Kate back a step while offering her hand. "Hello, I'm Sue. Won't you come in?"

"Thanks. I'm Drake." He stepped inside and shook Sue's hand.

"This is Kelsie and Missy. You obviously already know Kate."

"Yes I do." His voice was soft as he spoke. "Are you ready to go, Kate?"

She swallowed hard and replied, "Yes, I am. I'm sorry I seemed so startled when I opened the door, Mr. Hampton. It's just when Mr. Denison insisted on sending someone to get me, I was expecting one of the regular company drivers, not a Vice President."

"So you're the new VP?" Sue smiled. "Well, it's very nice to meet you, Drake. I have to say though, you're not quite what I expected from Kate's description."

His eyebrow rose and he cocked his head. "What were you expecting?"

Kate looked at her watch. "It's past six-thirty. Shouldn't we be going?"

Drake grinned. "I'll let you off the hook this time." He waved a hand and said good evening to her friends as he escorted her out the door.

*****

Stay calm, he's just a man. Stay calm, he's just a man. Stay calm, he's just a man. Kate kept repeating the phrase in her head as she walked to the car. Drake opened the door for her. She watched as he walked around and slid behind the wheel. He didn't speak until they were out on the road. "I don't really know many places around here yet, but Bill suggested we try the Lakeside Chalet. He said they have good food and it's quiet so we can talk."

Kate started to get an uneasy feeling in the pit of her stomach. She knew the restaurant, it was known for its fabulous cuisine and intimate atmosphere. The kind of place couples went for a romantic evening, not business dinners. Drake, of course, wouldn't know that, but she thought Bill would have.

Kate swallowed hard. "How many people are going to be there?"

"Didn't Bill tell you? I decided to talk to everyone individually. I find people are often more candid one on one than they are in a group of their peers. So it will just be the two of us this evening."

Don't hyperventilate, don't hyperventilate, don't hyperventilate, her mind chanted as she concentrated on taking long slow breaths.

When they entered the restaurant, she made her excuses and went to the ladies room. She looked in the mirror and berated herself. "Calm down. There is no reason to be this nervous. He's just a man." She took three slow, deep breaths. "Pull yourself together and be professional. This is a business dinner." After three more deep breaths, she felt better. Now that she was past the shock of the situation she felt like she could get through the rest of the evening. She wished she could figure out what it was about this man that had her strung so tight. She didn't think it was his position in the company. She frequently talked to the president and the other two VP's without reacting like this.

*****

While Drake waited for her, he couldn't believe he finally had her all to himself. He had purposely avoided her all week, having too much work to get done to be distracted. And she was defiantly a distraction. It had been hard to keep his mind on his job just knowing she was in the same building.

He would have to be sure and thank Bill again for suggesting this dinner. He knew Kate thought this was strictly a business dinner. Although he did have some tooling questions for her, he saw no reason for the entire evening to revolve around work. There were too many other things he wanted to know about her. Such as, what she liked to do for fun, how she spent her evenings, what were her plans for the future, was her hair as silky as it looked, were her lips as soft as he imagined...

She emerged from the hallway then, and they were shown to a quiet corner table overlooking the lake. The lighting was soft and low. A small candle flickered between them. Drake thought it was perfect.

She wasn't as fidgety as she had been, but wasn't completely at ease either.

"Is something wrong?"

"No. I'm sorry, this is just a little strange for me. I don't normally do business dinners. This isn't exactly what I was expecting."

Drake smiled. "I get tired of stuffy offices and drab conference rooms. I thought this would be more enjoyable. We can discuss work over a nice meal in a relaxing atmosphere." He picked up his menu and browsed through it. "So what looks good to you?"

Kate hid behind the menu. "I can't decide between the grilled salmon or the peppercorn steak. Both sound really good." She decided on the steak. Drake ordered the Prime rib.

During the meal, Drake gently probed her for personal information. Finding out how long she had worked at Denetech, where she grew up, about the friends he had met. He would occasionally volunteer information about himself trying to keep the conversation casual. When he asked about her house her face softened, and for the first time that evening she relaxed and spoke freely. She told him what she went through to be able to get it. How hard she had worked and how long it had taken. About how wonderful it was when she finally achieved her goal.

"You don't mind living by yourself?"

"No. Not at all."

"Don't you ever get lonely?"

"Not really. Missy, Kelsie, and Sue don't give me much chance to be lonely."

"They spend a lot of time there. I take it."

"Kelsie is married now and Missy is engaged, so I don't see them quite as often as I used to but they still manage to come over once or twice a week. Sue practically lives there some weeks."

"Where does she normally live?"

"She has an apartment in town. She doesn't like living alone, but says it puts a cramp in her style to have a roommate. So keeping her own apartment and spending time at my house whenever she wants gives her the best of both worlds."

"Doesn't it cramp your style to have her popping in and out of your place whenever she wants?"

Kate laughed. A sound he would like to hear more often. "No. If you ask my friends they'd tell you I don't have a style to cramp."

"Surely you date. A woman as beautiful as you can't possibly work around so many men and not have them standing in line to ask you out."

She was instantly fidgety again and blushed deep enough he could see it clearly even as low as the lighting was. "Actually, I don't go out much. I do work with a lot of men, but I've known most of them for so long it would be strange to date them. I hang out at Pete's with them sometimes. We play darts and shoot pool. I'm just considered one of the guys."

He watched her until she glanced up at him. "I had gotten the impression most of the men in the shop were quite intelligent, but if they think of you as one of the guys I may have to rethink my position."

She swallowed hard and when she spoke her voice cracked. "Speaking of the shop," She took a sip of water. "You wanted to discuss the tool crib, didn't you?" Her voice was a bit more steady this time. Obviously she wanted to get back to less personal topics. He was willing to give on that, but he wasn't anywhere near ready to have this evening over yet.

"Yes, I do have a few questions." He pushed his empty plate aside. "Are you finished?" He pointed to her plate.

"Yes, I am."

"Good." He waved toward their server and asked for the check. When that was paid, Drake stood up and stepped beside her. "Shall we?" he said, motioning to the door.

"Where are we going?"

"Not many people know this, but I have a terrible sweet tooth. I've been dying to try that coffeehouse ever since you told me about it. You can show me where it is and we can talk shop over dessert.

Chapter Three

Drake held the car door as she slid in. He was glad she didn't seem as nervous this time as she had earlier when he'd picked her up. As they drove the six miles to Pierceton, Kate told him about the coffeehouse.

"Mick, the owner, is very unique. Most people's first impression is that he's kind of a sixties throw back. He drives a van painted in true flower power style. Complete with bright colors, large flowers, and a peace sign covering most of the back end. He has shoulder length hair, and a full beard. He's very laid back and just wants to have a place where people can come and enjoy themselves. He keeps board games and cards on hand for people to use, or you can bring your own. There's a smaller room in the back lit mainly with candles where they have live music on the weekends. Not full bands or anything. Usually just one to three people who come in and play guitar and sing bluegrass or old pop songs."

"The main room is where you find what seems like a bizarre contradiction. Many people of the flower child mindset protested against war and didn't want to have anything to do with it. Except for the back room, the coffeehouse is scattered with civil war memorabilia. Mick travels with a group that does civil war reenactments. Coats, helmets, uniforms, powder horns, he has a whole collection hanging on coat hooks on every wall of the main room."

Drake noticed as she spoke she started to relax again. He wasn't surprised after hearing about the owner of the coffeehouse that she liked the place so much. She was kind of a bizarre contradiction herself. She worked with over a hundred men everyday without flinching. He had personally watched her stand her ground with a man more than twice her size. It was obvious talking to the men she was a highly respected member of the team. He had watched from across the shop as she dealt with lines of impatient men waiting on supplies without getting rattled. On the other hand, she seemed extremely uncomfortable to be alone with one man, or have a situation turn personal. *Hopefully that will change.* It would take time, but it would change.

He maneuvered into a parking place and turned off the engine. From the outside he would have never guessed this was a coffeehouse. He pushed open the old wooden door and let her go through. The inside was just as she had described. Kate walked over to a large glass case where the desserts were displayed.

"What do you recommend?" Drake peered over her shoulder.

"It's all good. It's always difficult to decide."

"Hey man, how's it goin'?" The owner said when he saw Kate.

"Great. We came in for dessert."

"Let me know what you decide on. I'll serve it up for ya."

They made their selection and found a table. Mick brought the dessert laden plates and drinks out. He stayed and chatted a few minutes, then wandered over to visit at another table. Kate took a bite of the pastry loaded with feather light mousse and shaved white chocolate. Drake's mouth went dry as she closed her eyes and rolled the delicacy around on her tongue.

"This is fantastic." She picked up a chunk of white chocolate from her plate and smiled. "Mick knows I love white chocolate so he always puts an extra piece on my plate. It pays to be a good customer."

Drake took a bite of his raspberry cheesecake and was impressed at how good it really was.

"Now," Kate said. "What do you want to know about the tool crib?"

They talked about work and he watched as she relaxed and obviously felt more at ease. Work was where she was in her element. Drake was impressed with her knowledge not only of the tools and fixtures, but the over all production process.

*****

An hour later, against her better judgment, she let him talk her into ordering a second dessert when he did. From there they went into stories of on the job goofs and mishaps they had seen or experienced. She laughed harder than she had in a long time. Catching her breath, she took a bite of white chocolate cheesecake and moaned. She stabbed another bite and held her fork out to him. "Here, you have to try this, it's incredible."

Drake leaned forward staring into her eyes as his lips closed around the cheesecake. Kate's breath caught in her throat. She had no idea what had possessed her to do such a thing. She and her friends often sampled each other's food or shared desserts when they ate out, but they didn't feed it to each other.

Drake slid his fingers over hers as he guided the fork from his mouth. "You're right, it is incredible."

"I'm terribly sorry. I... I can't believe I just did that. That was definitely not a very business-like thing to do."

His eyes were still locked with hers as he replied, "I don't mind if you're not all business."

She looked away. Trying to cover her embarrassment she forced a grin and picked up a small piece of white chocolate. "It must be this. Some people have alcohol, others have drugs, I have white chocolate. It causes me to do uncharacteristic things."

Drake leaned toward her sliding his hand over hers once again, "I'll have to remember that."

She carefully extracted her hand and looked at her watch. She was amazed to discover it was almost midnight. "I had no idea it was so late. I really should be getting home."

Drake paid the bill and Kate said goodbye to Mick as they left. Once in the car, Kate became quiet. This was not a date, but the thought of that awkward end of the evening moment still made her uneasy.

It had sure seemed more like a date than a business dinner. Except for those few tense moments right before they left the restaurant, and again before leaving the coffeehouse, she had actually relaxed and enjoyed herself. He was a brilliant conversationalist, discussing a wide variety of topics. He had a fantastic sense of humor and was not afraid to laugh at himself. If she wasn't careful she could develop some pretty strong feelings for him. That, of course, could only lead to trouble. He was a Vice President. He might enjoy a business dinner with her, even flirt with her a little, but they weren't on the same playing field. Even if they were, a relationship wasn't in the cards for her, she needed to remember that.

Kate was listening to the low volume of the radio when one of her favorite love songs began to softly play. She leaned her head back and let her eyes drift shut for a moment. She heard Drake start to quietly hum, then softly sing the words. The sound wrapped around her like a cocoon. She would never be able to listen to the song again without hearing his voice.

When they reached her drive Drake got out and, much to Kate's relief, left the engine running. She didn't think he would want to come in, but nothing about this evening had gone the way she thought it would. He walked her to the door and waited while she unlocked it. He took her hand and murmured, "Now it's my turn to do something that's definitely not very business-like." He leaned toward her, softly brushing his lips against hers, and whispered, "Sweet dreams, Kate" then was gone. She let herself into the house as he strolled back to his car.

Kate stumbled into the kitchen a few minutes past ten the next morning. She normally didn't sleep so late, but she had been awake until the wee hours of the morning. She'd tossed and turned most of the night not being able to get Drake off her mind. Sue's voice startled her. "Good morning, sleepy head."

Sue, Missy, and Kelsie were all sitting at the kitchen table. "Don't you people have homes of your own?" Kate grumbled.

"Sure we do," Sue answered. "But we had to come over and get the scoop."

"What scoop?" Kate asked, dropping bread into the toaster.

"What do you mean what scoop?" Sue stood up exasperated. "How did it go with the VP last night?"

"Fine." She retrieved apple butter and milk from the refrigerator.

All three of them glared at her. "Look," Missy said. "I would love to tell you we don't want to pry and it's none of our business, but we all know that would be a lie. You know as well as we do none of us are going to leave you alone until we have every detail of what happened last night, so why don't you make it easy on yourself and just tell us now."

Kate took a long drink of milk and sighed. "It was just a business dinner. He had some questions about the tool crib and I answered them. That was pretty much it."

"If that was it, why were you still not home at midnight when I came by on my way back from John's?" Missy asked. "That's an awfully long business dinner."

Kelsie stepped in. "Where was the dinner at?"

Kate knew she was had now. If she told them where they had gone she would never hear the end of it. She also knew Missy had spoken the truth when she said they wouldn't leave her alone. Either way they would make her life miserable for a while. She took a deep breath. "It was at the Lakeside Chalet."

"You went there for a business dinner?" Sue asked suspiciously. "How many people were there?"

"There were two of us."

"Two of you, as in, two of you meeting with Drake, or two of you, as in, just you and Drake?"

Kate bit into her toast, giving herself a moment of delay before answering. "It was just me and Drake."

"Well, that must have been cozy." Sue smiled.

"John and I go to the Lakeside Chalet sometimes. It closes at eleven. So where were you until after midnight?"

Kate finished her milk before letting out a long exasperated breath. She walked her dishes over to the sink. Eventually she turned and looked at her friends. They were all watching her intently. Too tired to argue she finally gave in.

"Drake is new in town and doesn't really know the area yet. Someone told him the Lakeside Chalet was quiet and had good food so he figured it would be a good place to talk. After dinner he asked me if I would mind going to the Mocha and Mousse. He heard they had great desserts, but he wasn't sure where it was and asked if I'd show him." She omitted the part about her being the one to tell him about the coffeehouse. "We had dessert and talked awhile, then he dropped me off here." She looked at Missy. "We must have just missed you because I got home about ten minutes after midnight. End of story." They all eyed her suspiciously.

Missy was the first one to speak. "So do you think he'll ask you out again?"

"He didn't ask me out this time. It was a business meeting Mr. Denison set up, not a date." She let out a long sigh. "I'm not going to pretend I had a lousy time because I didn't. I really enjoyed last night. He's intelligent and funny and, yes, even I noticed how good-looking he is. But I enjoy spending time with lots of guys from work without any intentions of dating them." She shrugged her shoulders. "This is no different."

Except none of the guys from work ever made her skin tingle, or caused her to stop breathing just by touching her hand. She had never gone to a romantic restaurant with one of them alone, and not one of them had ever kissed her. Other than that, it really was no different, she assured herself.

Although still skeptical, her friends let the subject drop for the moment.

Kate spent a quiet weekend at home reading and watching old movies. She was glad when Monday morning came and she could get back to work and keep busy. It started as a hectic morning, but after a couple of hours, slowed to a manageable pace. Just before lunch she heard dramatic high-pitched 'oohs' and 'ahhs' coming from the shop along with howls and wolf whistles. She smiled knowing exactly what was causing it. Now and then a wife or girlfriend would send one of the men balloons or flowers for a special occasion. The poor guy on the receiving end would be teased relentlessly for the rest of the day. The bell rang and she was not surprised to see Cindy, the lobby receptionist standing at the window. Other than the occasional delivery, she didn't come out to the shop floor. Since Production people came and went through an employee entrance at the back of the building Cindy really didn't know many of the men. She usually stopped and asked Kate where she could find the recipient.

Kate gave a low whistle. "Wow, someone must have had a great weekend," she said looking at the huge arrangement of two dozen dark red roses and a box wrapped in satiny white paper with delicately embossed roses. "Who's the lucky guy?"

"Actually they're not for a guy. They're for you."

Kate laughed. "Nice try. Who are they really for?"

Cindy turned the flowers so Kate could see the card. There in bold script was her name. Kate stood dumbfounded staring at the card.

"Would you take these please? They're getting heavy."

Kate closed her mouth and opened the small door knowing she couldn't get the tall vase and flowers through the window without breaking the stems or dumping the water. Cindy handed her the roses and the box, and smiled. "Enjoy the rest of your day."

Kate closed the door and walked back to her desk. She set the flowers and package down and opened the small envelope. *Thanks for a lovely evening, Drake* was written on the card. She stared at the box afraid to open it. Finally she took a deep breath and untied the ribbon. Slowly tipping back the lid she saw another card lying on tissue paper. Her hand shook slightly as she opened it. *For our next dinner* was written on this one. She pulled back the tissue paper to reveal a pound of white chocolate. Her face immediately flushed at the implication. She slammed the lid back down on the box.

"That good? Or that bad?" The voice startled her. Kate spun around to find eight sets of eyes looking at her.

"Wh... What?" She stammered, holding the cards against her chest.

"You blushed when you opened it, then slammed the lid shut. It was either something really good, or really bad." The man wriggled his eyebrows. "So which is it?" Terry appeared to have taken on the role of spokesman for the group.

"It's um, I ah...Don't you guys have work to do?" she asked, sliding the box back against the wall and out of their sight.

"Sure we do, but you know flowers are always big news around here. So who sent them? Anyone we know?"

"Like it's any of your business." She slid both cards into her pocket, making sure nobody could sneak in and find them. Kate knew there were a few men out there who were not past doing just that.

"Come on, you can tell us. We won't tell anybody, honest." The guys all raised their right hands and crossed their hearts with the left. That was her undoing and she burst out laughing.

"You guys gossip worse than a bunch of old ladies. There's no way I'm telling you anything."

Terry looked stricken. "I can't believe you don't trust us. I'd tell you who it was if I got flowers."

Kate laughed again. "No kidding," she said sarcastically. "If a woman ever sent you flowers you'd have it announced in sky writing above the shop." All the other guys agreed laughingly.

"That was low," Terry feigned anguish. "I'll have you know I have to fight the women off."

One of the other men laughed. "Yeah, he has to fight 'em off alright. He has to fight to get away from them when they try to slap him senseless."

"I'm going back to by machine," announced Terry amongst the laughter, throwing his nose in the air, trying his best to look offended. "I don't have to stand here and take this abuse." He turned around and marched to his machine.

When the others disbursed, Kate stood staring at the roses. Nobody had ever sent her flowers before, let alone roses. She wasn't sure what to think about the gesture. Maybe it was simply meant to be a thank you for taking the time to answer his questions. Although she hadn't noticed him sending roses and chocolate to anyone else he had talked to. Before she had time to come to any conclusions the lunch bell rang. She opened the bottom desk drawer to get her purse when the phone rang. Two short rings meant it was a call from inside the building. Kate considered not answering it. There were those in the building who considered their needs much more important than her lunch break. On the third ring, however, she gave in and answered it.

"Tool crib."

"Hello, Kate." The now familiar voice vibrated through her.

"Hello, Mr. Hampton."

She heard his soft chuckle. "I thought we were past formal names."

"Is there something I can help you with?"

"I just wanted to tell you how much I enjoyed the other night."

"You already did that." Her voice softened. "Thank you for the flowers. They're beautiful."

"I'm glad you like them. I am also glad you're being so gracious about them. I was afraid you either wouldn't accept them or you'd give me one of those you really shouldn't have speeches."

"I figure we both already know you shouldn't have so I decided not waste my breath. And despite the reputation I have around here, not even I could refuse such gorgeous roses. So I decided to simply enjoy them for their natural beauty and not ruin it by making a scene."

"Did you get the chocolate as well?"

She slid into her chair and drew her knees up propping her feet on the open drawer. "Yes I did, but I'm not going to thank you for it. That was just plain mean," she said, grinning. It was strange, but somehow talking to him on the phone was easier than face to face.

"Mean? Why was it mean?"

"Do you have any idea how dangerous it is to give that much chocolate to a woman who lives alone? With no one to hold me accountable for how much I eat, don't be surprised when I call in sick tomorrow with a chocolate hangover."

She closed her eyes and listened to the deep throaty laugh. His voice became soft and sensual. "I would hate to think I was responsible for making you sick. Maybe I should come over and spend the evening with you so I can make sure you're safe."

Kate felt color flood her cheeks. She hadn't meant for that to be an invitation. "I'd be safer alone with the chocolate." She also hadn't meant for that to be out loud.

"Why do you say that?"

She swiveled slightly in her chair twirling the phone cord around her finger when a movement caught her eye. A group of men stood by the window leaning on the fence, eating popcorn, and watching her. "Oh no," she groaned.

"What's wrong?"

"I've just become the floor show."

"What?"

"I really have to go."
"I'll call you this evening."
"There's no need for that."
"Yes there is. I'll talk to you later, Kate."

She hung up the phone glad her desk was too far from the window for anyone to have heard her end of the conversation. Looking at her watch she noted there was still enough time to grab lunch. She pulled her purse out of the drawer and walked toward the group. "Is there something you need?" She opened the door.

"Not really," one of the men replied. "We were just enjoying the show. I take it from the smiles and giggles you were talking to the person who sent the flowers."

"I'm hungry, if you'll excuse me I'm going to get something to eat."

"Oh, come on, Kate, tell us who they're from. Are you serious about him? Is he from around here? Give us something."

"What I'll give you is dull tooling from now on if you don't leave me alone. Did you ever think maybe they're from my grandmother to thank me for helping her move last month?"

"Yeah, right. Women don't blush and get all doe eyed and giggly over a grandmother."

"Doe eyed and giggly?" Kate's stomach knotted as she heard Drake's voice.

"Hi, Drake. We were just trying to find out who sent Kate flowers and the box that made her blush," Smitty offered, "But she won't tell us. She was just feeding us some line about them being from her grandmother."

Kate gave Smitty a look that would have withered most people, but he had known her too long to be afraid of her. "I'm going to lunch." she grated as she pushed past the crowd.

Watching her leave, another member of the group spoke. "Wow, maybe it finally happened."

"What?" Drake inquired.

"Maybe she's finally met someone that broke through. In all the years we've known her, she has never had a boyfriend that we know of. When she started here some of the guys asked her out, but she always turned them down, telling them she didn't want the complication of dating someone from work. Later we got to know some of her friends and found out she just doesn't date at all. If she has found someone, I hope for his sake he deserves her."

Drake's brows furrowed. "What do you mean?" he asked carefully.

The man laughed. "Kate is very well liked around here. She has always fit right in. More times than we can count she has gone out of her way to help any number of us. Professionally and personally. She doesn't get offended when one of us is in a bad mood and says something we shouldn't. She's definitely not some floozy a guy could just mistreat and get away with it. You might say if word got out some guy hurt her there would be a very long line of men wanting to know his name."

"I'd be first in line," Smitty said.

Drake looked up at the man he'd seen Kate yell at that first day. He had never considered himself a wimp, but he wouldn't leap in front of a moving train to try and stop it either. He glanced at Smitty again and considered himself duly warned.

Steve looked at Drake. "We wouldn't let him go first. There wouldn't be anything left for the rest of us if he did." The men all laughingly agreed as they went their separate ways.

Instead of being worried, Drake felt his feelings for Kate grow even stronger. He'd heard the way some of the men talked about other single women in the building. It often wasn't very flattering. He knew others were well liked, but it was obvious Kate had earned a special place in the shop.

*****

As Kate was getting ready to leave for the day, Mr. Denison stopped by the cage, leaning on her desk. "Hi Kate. How are you today?"

"I'm fine thanks. How is your day going?"

"Not bad for a Monday. Did you have a nice weekend?"

"Yes."

He picked up a pencil and studied it. "So how did your dinner with Drake turn out?" He asked casually. A little too casually.

"It went well I guess. I think I managed to answer most of his questions about the tool crib."

"I've known Drake a long time. What do you think of him?"

"He seems to know his stuff. The people in production really like him. I think they like the fact he's trying to learn how things are done and is genuinely asking for input and not just coming in and trying to take over. People tend to respect that."

Bill studied her for a moment. "That's nice to know, but I didn't ask what everyone else thinks of him. I asked what you think of him."

Kate started to fidget not sure how to answer. "I think I really don't know him that well. I think from what I've seen, he'll be a good asset to the company."

Bill looked at the roses. "Nice flowers."

"Yes."

"Any special occasion?"

Her response was guarded. "Just a thank you."

He grinned. "My dear, a note or a phone call is a thank you. A small arrangement of spring flowers possibly, but a man doesn't send two dozen dark red long stem roses and a gift unless he means business." He chuckled when she blushed and patted her shoulder adding, "Drake is a good man."

She had started to suspect before, but now she knew. "You set me up." her disbelief obvious.

"Now my dear, Drake did need to talk to you, and you have to admit, it would be difficult during work hours. I didn't see any reason why the two of you couldn't discuss work over a nice dinner." He gave her a quick wink. "I didn't have anything to do with the flowers though. That was strictly Drake's doing. By the looks of things, you made quite an impression."

"You set me up," she repeated, still stunned. If her friends had tricked her into a date or someone in production had set her up with somebody as a joke, she wouldn't have been so surprised. Bill, however, was the CEO of the company. And he had set her up with a VP!

A buzzer rang in the shop signaling the end of the shift. Kate, still in shock, picked up her purse and walked toward the door. "Kate." Bill called after her. "You forgot your flowers." He stood up and chuckled as he left through the back door.

Chapter Four

That evening Kate fixed herself a quick supper and soaked in the tub for an hour. She slipped into a nightshirt and curled up on the couch in front of the TV. The kitchen door opened and Sue yelled her name. "I'm in here," she answered, not bothering to get up.

Sue came strolling in a minute later with a satisfied smirk on her face. "Should I ask who the roses are from, or would you like me to guess?"

"Give me a break I've been harassed enough for one day."

"Okay I won't harass you about the flowers. I do have to wonder though, how he found out about your white chocolate fetish. It usually takes years for a man to learn even the simplest personal details about you. Yet Drake found out your biggest weakness on the first date. How exactly did that come about?"

Just then the phone rang. Kate rolled face down on the couch and groaned. "I don't suppose you'd be willing to answer that and say I'm not home."

"No, I wouldn't."

"Okay, then I'll let the machine get it."

Sue jumped up and grabbed the phone. Kate listened to the one sided conversation. "Hello. Hi, Drake, this is Sue. I'm fine. Yes, she's here, I'll get her for you." Sue held the phone out. "It's for you. I'd love to stay, but I know if I had a guy like Drake is on the line I'd want a little privacy so I'll leave you two alone."

Kate sat up and took the phone. She held her hand over it and took a deep breath as Sue scooted out the door. Bringing the phone to her ear, she said, "Hello."

"Hi, Kate."

"Hello, Drake. Is something wrong at work?"

"Not that I'm aware of. The reason I'm calling doesn't have anything to do with work."

Kate closed her eyes. "Why are you calling?"

"We didn't get to finish our conversation today."

"We didn't?"

"No, we didn't. I'm confused by a couple of things you said."

"Which things would that be?"

"First, you said we both know I shouldn't have sent the flowers. I want to know why you think I shouldn't have. Second, I'd like to know what you meant when you said you'd be safer with the chocolate than with me."

"I don't suppose we could do this some other time. I've had a rough day and am not thinking too clearly right now."

"We could do it over dinner tomorrow," he offered.

"Then again, maybe now isn't such a bad time after all." She sighed. "Look, it was really nice of you to send me flowers. I just think it was inappropriate. I didn't notice you sending flowers to anybody else at work after talking to them." Kate ran a hand through her hair. "As for the other thing, people are already trying to find out who sent the flowers. If they found out it was you they would make my life miserable. The rumor mill at work has a life of its own. If we were seen together and my name got linked with yours it would be terrible. I've seen what such rumors as secretaries and their bosses, or copy girls and supervisors have done to a few people. I can't imagine what kind of havoc the tool crib attendant and the Vice President would cause. It's bad enough my friends saw you the other night. They're still not finished badgering me about our dinner."

His voice slid into that soft sensual tone again. "Well then we better start coming up with a plan."

"A plan for what?"

"A plan for how we're going to see each other without the rumors getting out of control. I want to see you Kate, and not just at work in passing."

Kate's heart skipped a beat. Her lungs constricted and she couldn't breathe.

"Kate?"

She forced air into her lungs and tried to form some sort of rational thought. "Yes I, ah..." Her voice cracked and she cleared her throat. "I'm flattered really." She swallowed hard and continued. "It's just not a good idea. You're new in town and don't know anybody here yet. I understand if you're feeling lonely and want someone to spend time with. We had dinner together and it was nice, but that doesn't mean we should see each other. If you'd like I could introduce you to some of my friends. Like Sue for instance, she loves to go out and have fun. She knows lots of people. She could help you have a full social life in no time and--"

"Kate." She was startled into silence. "I'm not lonely or lacking for a social life. Nor do I want to go out with Sue. I have nothing against her, but she's not the one I want to spend time with. I would like to get to know you better. I don't mind keeping a low profile for now if it makes you more comfortable."

Kate was surprised to find she was almost in tears. She must be more tired than she thought, and getting overly emotional. "I don't think it's a very good idea."

"I think it's a very good idea." he said with a self-assured laugh. "I know you've had a long day so I won't keep you any longer. I'll see you tomorrow." Before she could hang up, she heard him softly call her name.

"Kate?"

"Yes?" she whispered.

"Sweet dreams."

She heard a soft click on the line and he was gone. She replaced the receiver and sat hugging her pillow.

Kate was again awake half the night tossing and turning trying to convince herself Drake hadn't meant what he said. An hour before her alarm was set to go off, she woke from a dream. The most erotic dream she'd ever had. Unlike most of her dreams, she could remember this one in vivid detail. Even now that she was awake it still felt real. Her body tingled and her breathing labored. If she closed her eyes she could feel Drake there.

She threw back the covers and climbed out of bed. Walking into the bathroom, she caught sight of her reflection in the mirror. Her face was flushed and her eyes were puffy and underscored with dark circles. "I can't believe you're letting a man do this to you." She grimaced. "Not only do you look terrible, but you've started talking to yourself on a regular basis." She shook her head and turned on the shower. "I must be going insane."

After her shower she was cleaner, but didn't really look any better. Of course few at work were tactful enough not to mention it. "Wow, you look terrible." Or "Rough night?" followed by winks and smirks were the most common statements she endured all morning. After she barked at enough of them they decided she'd had enough and left her alone. It was the longest day she remembered ever having since starting at Denetech. It wasn't simply the comments and questions, or even the fact she was dead tired. It was the fear Drake could come by at any minute and she would have to face him. By lunch time she almost wished he would come by and get it over with so she could stop worrying about it. Her entire shift passed, however, with no sign of him.

Relieved to be home where she was safe she finally relaxed. She was hungry, but decided she needed a nap more than food. She woke an hour later feeling somewhat groggy. After a long stretch and a yawn it was definitely time to eat.

As she left her bedroom familiar voices drifted down the hall along with a welcomed aroma. "I smell pizza, I hope there's some left," she said as she entered the room trying to rub the gritty feeling from her eyes. "I'm starved." Kate walked to the cupboard beside the stove, stretching up on tiptoe to retrieve a box of tea bags from the top shelf. "What kind is it?" She filled the teakettle with water and set it on the stove.

Suddenly she realized it was much too quiet. An uneasy feeling crept up her spine. The friends she knew were never quiet. Slowly she turned and looked toward the table. There sat Sue, Missy, Kelsie, and Drake. Her eyes locked with his. "What are you doing here?"

"I heard you had a rough day so I brought pizza. There's also chips and soda."

"He was thoughtful enough to bring extra in case we were here," said Sue. "Isn't he a nice guy?"

Kate knew Sue was trying to get a rise out of her. "Yes, isn't he," she agreed sarcastically. Kate opened another cupboard and started to reach for a cup.

"You might want to rethink stretching for another top shelf," Kelsie said.

Kate turned, "Why?" Kelsie looked slightly embarrassed, Missy giggled, and Sue had a Cheshire cat grin on her face. It wasn't until she caught Drake's look and comment, however, understanding dawned on her.

She stood immobile as his gaze traveled the length of her, then returned to lock with hers. With a soft voice and inviting grin, he said, "I don't mind if she gets herself a cup."

Kate looked down remembering she had changed into a nightshirt before her nap. It wasn't bad enough her bottom half was only covered to about mid thigh, the shirt she had picked was missing a button that left a very deep V of her top half exposed as well. Kate had blushed many times in her life, but this was the first time it was so severe her ears burned and her temples throbbed. She turned without a word and walked back to her room. She closed the door and leaned against it a moment hoping to calm her rattled nerves. When the solitude of her room helped ease her tension, she stepped over and dropped down on the bed. She was still sitting there when she heard a soft knock on the door. She didn't respond, hoping whoever it was would go away, but seconds later the door slowly opened. Drake walked over and offered her a cup of tea. Kate took it without looking up as he sat beside her on the bed. She sipped the hot liquid while he arranged her nightstand to accommodate the tray he'd also brought with him. He cut a bite of pizza and held the fork to her mouth.

"Here, I know you're hungry."

Tired and hungry, a feeling of defeat washed over her and she took what was offered.

They sat quietly as she finished the pizza. When it was gone he set the plate on the nightstand and gently pulled her onto his lap. He placed a hand on her head drawing it down to his shoulder. She sighed and relaxed against him too drained to fight.

She hadn't felt such an overwhelming need to cry in years. She had managed to keep her life on a very even plain for a long time, and now it was all falling apart. She was no longer used to such emotional turmoil. She didn't know what to cry about first. The fact Drake had disrupted

A Dream to be Loved

her serenity? That her friends and even the CEO were conspiring against her? The fear of people at work finding out? Or the worst thing of all, that some part of her wanted to give in to what she was feeling.

It felt so good to be in his arms. He was warm and strong, he smelled of outdoors and after-shave. She had been alone for so long, the idea of having someone to lean on was incredibly tempting. Someone to laugh with, to go out with, to curl up in the evenings with. Someone who would hold her when she had a bad day, to kiss her when...

Kate lifted her head and slid off his lap. "Thanks for the pizza. It was good. If you'll excuse me I need to get dressed."

Drake stood up and softly kissed her forehead. "I'll wait for you in the kitchen." He picked up the empty dishes and carried them out of the room, closing the door behind him.

*****

Kate's friends were still at the table when Drake returned to the kitchen.

"I'm glad to see you're still in one piece," Sue observed. "I wasn't sure how you'd be received back there."

"I wasn't either," he admitted. "I think she'll be out in a minute."

"Well," Missy said. "I believe we all have somewhere else to be. Thanks for the pizza, Drake."

The three stood and gathered their things. Sue walked over to Drake and held out a piece of paper. "Here, in case you run out of ideas and need help. She's very cautious, and can be irritatingly stubborn, but if you're willing to stick it out you won't find a more incredible woman."

Drake took the paper and unfolded it. It contained the names and phone numbers of the three women in the room. "I realized she was an incredible woman the moment I met her." He held up the paper. "Thanks, I really appreciate this." They filed out the door, but before Sue was all the way out she turned, "Drake?"

"Yes?"

"We're crossing our fingers for you, but I should warn you. If you hurt her, your life won't be worth living. Have a nice evening." She smiled as she pulled the door shut behind her.

Drake shook his head. He had never had his life threatened before. Since meeting Kate, however, it seemed as if one false move would have the whole world gunning for him. He looked toward the hall. He'd be willing to bet she wasn't even aware of the kind of love and protectiveness she produced in those who knew her. He stowed the leftover pizza and chips and was wiping the counter when Kate emerged. She looked around cautiously.

"The others left," he stated.

Kate walked to the stove. "I'm going to make more tea. Would you like some?"

"No, thank you."

Neither spoke as she went about her chore. When she was done she strolled into the living room and curled up on the couch. Drake sat next to her. This new mood of hers was strange. She didn't completely ignore him nor did she completely acknowledge him. Her indifference gave him the impression she resigned herself to accept him as an unavoidable presence. She turned on the TV and browsed the listings. "Do you like action movies?"

"Yes."

"There's one coming on."

"Sounds good to me. Do you have any popcorn?"

"There should be some in the pantry." She started to get up.

Drake placed a staying hand on her shoulder, "I'll make it, you stay put." He pulled the navy and white fleece throw off the back of the couch and covered her up. Ten minutes later, he was back with a bowl of popcorn and two cans of soda.

By the time the movie was over the popcorn and soda were gone. Drake got up and pulled Kate off the couch. "You look exhausted," he told her as he pulled her gently into his arms. "Thanks for the popcorn and movie." He lowered his head and kissed her softly before whispering, "Sweet dreams, Kate." Reluctantly, he released her and let himself out.

*****

Kate went through the motions of preparing for bed, sure, as tired as she was, sleep would come instantly. Instead Drake's kiss kept replaying in her mind. It had been quick, but soft and warm. A whirlwind of response spun through her, wreaking havoc with her senses. She moaned and rolled over. "I need to get some sleep." The more tired she got the more defenseless and vulnerable she would become. That would be dangerous. Her reaction to a simple goodnight kiss from Drake was much more intense, and unnerving, than it should be. If she let her defenses down enough for him to really kiss her, she knew she would be lost.

She crawled out of bed and headed to the bathroom down the hall. Opening the medicine cabinet, she immediately found what she was looking for. Sue occasionally took an over-the-counter sleep aid and had left a bottle here. Kate took half the recommended dose and went back to bed. "That jerk!" She yelled out loud. She never had trouble sleeping before and as far as she was concerned the fact that she did now was all his fault.

The next morning when Kate's alarm went off it startled her. She jumped and knocked it off the stand. She flopped back down on the mattress for a moment to catch her breath, then rolled over and retrieved the clock.

By the time she arrived at work she felt really good. It was amazing what a full eight hours worth of sleep could do for you. She felt ready for anything today. Which turned out to be a good thing because almost everything that could go wrong, did.

She'd been waiting a week for an order of dovetail cutters ground with a special radius. They were needed for a high priority job. They finally arrived, but turned out to have the wrong radius. A fixture someone needed for a mill had been issued out on third shift the week before and hadn't been returned. She spent an hour tracking it down, finally finding it on a cart back in the shipping department. An order of six-foot band saw blades had arrived, but the company that sent them had transposed the numbers and instead of receiving the eighteen she'd requested she ended up with eighty-one sitting on pallets outside the cage.

These mishaps stacked on top of the standard everyday routine kept her too busy to think about anything else. She had seen Drake out in the shop a few times. He appeared to be as busy as she was. She glanced out in the shop about two o'clock to find him looking at her. Their eyes met and locked for one intense moment until someone walked up to him and he looked away. Kate turned and took a deep breath. A single look shouldn't have her reacting this way. She rubbed a hand down her arm, hoping to smooth away the sensations he had caused.

Later that evening while convincing herself she was glad he hadn't shown up again tonight the phone rang. "Hello."

"Hi, Kate."

She looked down at her arms, the goose bumps were back.

"Hello, Drake."

"I called to let you know I've been stuck in a meeting all evening. We decided to take a short break for dinner. We'll be reconvening in a few minutes."

"You don't have to report your whereabouts to me."

"I didn't want you to think I'd forgotten about you." She could hear the humor in his voice.

"I'm not that lucky," she replied, but couldn't help a grin of her own.

"I heard about some of the problems you had today. Did you manage to get most of them straightened out?"

"Most of them? Well, I can see your confidence in me is lacking. Haven't you heard? I'm wonder woman of the tooling world. I got all of it straightened out. The excess saw blades have been shipped back, the correct dovetail cutters will be here in the morning via overnight shipping, and I found the lost fixture returning it to its rightful place. Not to mention sorted and shipped out an order of tools to be sharpened, relabeled the polishing supplies, issued and received the usual daily supplies, and removed three titanium shavings from Smitty's hand."

She closed her eyes and listened to Drake's soft chuckle. "Wow, you really are wonder woman." His voice lowered. "If I had a splinter, would you remove it for me?"

Her tone was soft and teasing. "That depends. Would you be as big of a baby about it as Smitty always is?"

"I take it Smitty doesn't like to have splinters removed?"

"I have to take him to the back of the cage so no one can watch. There's been a time or two I worried he would pass out."

He laughed again. "How is it you manage to turn even the biggest men into putty?"

"It's a gift," she quipped with her usual sarcastic tone "You looked pretty busy yourself today."

"Yes I was. And I'm glad to know you keep an eye on me too." Her breath caught as she realized she admitted to watching him, while he continued with the report of his day. "We were trying to iron out the bugs in two new programs. Besides that, there were six different rush orders running and one of the machines went down and had to be repaired."

"I don't envy you. I can't imagine having a day like today, then being stuck in meetings all evening. How do you stay awake?"

"Lots of coffee," His tone softened, "and daydreaming about you."

"Didn't anybody ever teach you that not every thought that comes into your head has to be verbalized?" was her exasperated reply.

He laughed openly. "Believe me, if I verbalized every thought I've had about you, your face would be a much darker shade of red than it is now."

It irritated her he knew his last comment had made her blush.

"I'm glad you were home. Talking to you has been the high point of my day."

"Boy, you must have had a bad day." She laughed.

"It looks like people are starting to gather in the conference room again so I'd better go." His tired sigh drifted across the line, then he whispered, "I wish I was there to kiss you goodnight." A tiny shiver ran up her spine. "Sweet dreams, Kate."

"Drake?"

"Yes?"

"I... goodnight."

"Goodnight."

With her heart racing Kate hung up the phone. The weariness in his voice had pulled at her. She found herself wanting to comfort him and had nearly asked him to stop by when his meeting ended. "You have got to get a grip. What is your problem all of the sudden?" She heaved a pillow across the room.

"Who are you yelling at?" Sue asked as she entered the room and looked around.

Kate rubbed her forehead. "I seem to have taken up talking to myself as a new hobby."

Sue sat down and propped her feet up on the coffee table. A broad grin crossing her face. "He really has you tied up in knots, doesn't he?" She laughed. "My, but how the mighty have fallen."

"Would it do any good to pretend I don't know who you're talking about?"

"No. Where is he tonight?"

"In a meeting at work."

"So has it reached the point where I should start ringing the doorbell before I come in?"

"No. Feel free to barge right in whenever you please like you always have."

"Okay, I will, but you be sure and let me know if the status changes."

"Of course, you'll be the first to know."

Chapter Five

Thursday evening, Drake knocked on her door. "Hi, Kate." He greeted as she answered the door.
"Hello, Drake. Come in." She stood back to let him pass.
"I didn't see any cars in the drive. Am I the only one here?"
"Yes, everybody else had plans for the evening." She couldn't stop the soft smile that often happened when she thought of her friends. "You'd never know I actually lived alone, would you? There are times it seems like my friends are here more than I am." He followed her into the kitchen. "I was just making supper. Have you eaten?"
"No, I haven't."
"Do you like cheese stuffed manicotti?"
"I love it. You make your own?"
Kate scowled as severely as she could without cracking a smile at the surprise in his tone. "Shocking I know, but I can cook."
He had the decency to look properly chastised for a moment, then gave her an impish grin. "Did I just blow my chance for a home cooked meal?"
She placed a finger on her chin and squinted at him. "Hmm, what a dilemma. On one hand, I feel the need to defend my cooking ability and let you stay. On the other hand, I'm not sure you deserve to sample such a culinary delight."
Trying his best to look apologetic, he said, "Would it help if I promised to never doubt your abilities again?"
"I suppose that will do." She sighed dramatically. "Okay, you can stay."
"Great. I rented a couple of movies. I thought if you were interested and didn't have any plans for this evening, we could watch one. I worked such long hours at my last job I didn't have much free time. There's a whole list of movies I've wanted to see, but haven't had the chance."
"Okay, I was just finishing up here. It will have to bake about thirty minutes. Would you rather wait until after we eat or start a movie now and eat in front of the TV when the food's done?"
"Either one is fine with me."
"I was going to fix a salad and garlic bread, too. I'll go ahead and do that then we can start a movie."
"Sounds good to me. Anything I can help with?"
"Sure. You can toss the salad while I work on the bread."

A Dream to be Loved

The two of them worked side by side talking about work and relating events of the day. Kate had tried hard to convince herself when he arrived she shouldn't let him stay. She had enjoyed living alone for the past few years. Relished the quiet evenings after a hectic day, the serenity of not having to deal with anybody during her off-hours unless she chose to. Lately however, she had started to dread the evenings alone. They had become longer and quieter somehow, especially now that Missy and Kelsie didn't visit as often.

There was nothing wrong with two people eating a meal and watching a movie together. It didn't mean they were involved. It just meant that two people who would otherwise spend a boring evening alone chose to keep each other company. Besides, it was nice to have someone to discuss work with who understood what she was talking about.

After she had properly justified her actions in her mind, she enjoyed the rest of the evening.

Drake's taste in movies varied as much as her own. He brought a comedy and a mystery. He listed some of the others he wanted to see. Suspense, action, and drama were all among those he named. "If you promise not to tell anyone and ruin my manly image, I'll also admit I occasionally enjoy a romantic flick."

Kate laughed. "I'll keep that secret for now. But I should warn you before you divulge anymore secrets, I'm not above the occasional use of blackmail when the need arises."

"Thanks for the warning. I'll remember that and try not to reveal anything too damaging. So which one do you want to see?"

"Let's watch this one," she said, handing him a DVD. "I love mysteries and this is one I haven't seen yet either."

When the stove timer rang, Kate paused the movie and went to the kitchen. Drake filled two salad bowls while she served the pasta and bread. Returning to the living room, she sat on the floor placing her dishes on the coffee table to eat, with Drake following suit.

When the movie was over and Drake finished his second helping of manicotti, he leaned back against the couch rubbing his stomach. "I will definitely never question your cooking abilities again. That was incredible."

"Thanks. Sorry I don't have anything to offer you for dessert."

"Believe me it's not a problem. I don't think I could eat another bite." After a long stretch and a yawn, he looked at his watch. "It's getting late, I'll help you clean up then I'll go so you can get some sleep." They both picked up their dishes and carried them to the kitchen. It didn't take long to load everything into the dishwasher and put away the food. Drake picked up his jacket and took Kate's hand leading her toward the door. When they reached it he turned to her and smiled. "It just occurred to me you said you didn't have anything for dessert. Is all the white chocolate gone?"

"No." she replied bluntly, "As I recall, I said I didn't have anything to offer you for dessert. I don't share white chocolate." She grinned unashamedly with one eyebrow cocked.

"Not even with me? I bought it," he replied in disbelief.

"I don't care who bought it, it's mine now." When he still didn't look convinced she said, "You know how close Missy, Kelsie, Sue and I are. They know any of them can come and go as they please and use anything here whenever they want. If they're in trouble they can call me anytime day or night, but nobody, not even one of them, touches my white chocolate. It's one of the two things I'm adamant about."

Taunting her, he said, "Wow, who would've guessed you have such a greedy, possessive streak."

"You can tease me all you want. It still won't get you any chocolate."

He laughed and stepped slightly closer. "So what's the other thing?" Her brow creased in confusion. "That you're adamant about?"

"Oh, my car. I don't let anyone drive my car."

He slid his arms around her and lowered his head. She held her breath and closed her eyes as his lips caressed hers. It was similar to the last kiss he had given her. It lasted slightly longer, but otherwise was the same. He raised his head and looked into her eyes.

"Thanks for the company. It was much nicer than spending another evening alone in my apartment. I'm already looking forward to next time." He brushed a lock of hair away from her face. "Sweet dreams, Kate."

Friday, the phone on Kate's desk rang mid-way through the day. "Hi, Kate, it's Drake," he announced, as if she wouldn't know that voice anywhere. "I just found out I have to go to Indianapolis for the weekend. The company down there that does heat treating for us is having trouble with some of our parts and needs someone to consult with. I have to go down and tie up a few loose ends anyway so I volunteered. I was hoping to take you out to dinner tonight, but it looks like it will have to be next week." His voice took on that low, smooth as velvet, tone that always left her nerve endings standing at attention. "Unless you'd like to come with me. My house is no longer available so we'd have to stay in a hotel. You'd have your own room, of course. Work shouldn't take up much of my time, then we'd have the rest of the weekend to enjoy the city."

Kate was glad he couldn't see her face when she realized how far her chin had dropped.

"Kate?"

"Lovely as that sounds," she retorted, "I have plans this weekend. So you go and have a good time."

He chuckled softly. "I'll make it up to you when I get back. I promise."

"You seem to be under the mistaken impression I'm disappointed by your being gone. I assure you, I don't have a problem with it. As far as I'm concerned there is nothing to make up."

"Okay, then I'll make it up to me when I get back, because I assure you, I do have a problem with being away from you for the weekend." She heard the smile in his voice at her exasperated sigh. "I have to leave right after lunch. I don't suppose I could talk you into coming to my office during your break so I can kiss you goodbye?"

Another irritated sound escaped her followed by; "No, I don't suppose you could."

"I could always come to the cage to get a kiss."

"Don't you dare!" She heard his laugh rumble across the line.

"I'll see you when I get back, Kate. I'll miss you this weekend."

"Have a nice trip," was all she said before they each hung up.

She was not going to miss him. She was glad he was going to be gone so she didn't have to wonder all weekend if and when he might show up. Most of all, she was not going to feel a pang of disappointment he hadn't said 'sweet dreams' to her. She didn't know him well enough to notice he always said the same thing as he left her.

Now that she had that little pep talk out of the way, she could get back to work.

Friday evening was the time Kate often did housework. She did some laundry, dusted, and vacuumed. After mopping the kitchen floor, she looked through the pantry and decided it was time for some shopping. Her friends often brought food over and there were times she ended up with an odd variation of things. Lots of odds and ends, but not much to make an actual meal. With so many people coming and going it was hard to keep up with what she had. She smiled. She could keep up with hundreds of supplies at work, but rarely knew what was in her own pantry.

Kate was tired by the time she returned home. Now she remembered why she normally did housework and not grocery shopping on Friday nights. The store was really crowded. Wanting something more fun to do she thought about the sketchpad she had seen earlier while cleaning. She used to love to draw, and had been quite good at it. Some people had encouraged her to look into it professionally, but she had always been afraid it would take the fun out of it. Drawing had always been very personal to her. Not something she shared with the world.

Walking to the hall closet, she retrieved the pad and her pencils. She doodled for awhile, then as she became more tired and her mind wandered, something started to take shape. She suddenly realized she had drawn Drake's face. She rarely drew people in any form; usually finding it difficult to get a good likeness. Looking at the picture in her lap, however, there was no mistaking who it was. She sat staring at her creation, debating whether to finish it or not. She didn't want to think about why this particular face had shown up on her paper. On the other hand, she had never done a better portrait. Eventually her hand started to move again. Carefully shading and shadowing, adding more detail to the features. Before long she was completely lost in the task again. Gradually working on the eyes. In past drawings, the eyes had been the easiest part of the face for her. Somehow though, it was the toughest part of this one. Drake had such depth in those gray eyes. So many different facets of his personality were held in them. Kate had witnessed many of them, the glint of humor, the intensity of concentration, the occasional glare of irritation. She had always found those amusing and somewhat attractive. It was some of his other looks that left her uneasy, the one that let her glimpse untold depths of passion. That serious look of intent when he wanted something from her, and the most frightening of all, that deep penetrating gaze when he made her feel as if he could see clear through to her inner core where she kept the most secret part of herself. The part she never shared with anybody.

When the drawing was done, she held it up and looked at it. Something about it bothered her, but she wasn't quite sure what. It was the first time her own artwork had surprised her. It was an incredible likeness considering her past work. She had even managed to capture something true to him in the eyes. So what was it about the picture leaving her so uncomfortable?

Deciding she was just tired, she picked up her supplies intending to go to bed. As she crossed the room she noticed the light blinking on her answering machine. She pushed the play button and heard Drake's quiet intimate tone. "Sweet dreams, Kate, and I hope they're of me."

A tear rolled down her cheek. "As if I've been able to dream of anything else lately," she told the machine.

Monday evening she wasn't surprised when Drake showed up. She hadn't seen him at work, but heard he was there. She absolutely did not wonder why he hadn't stopped by the cage or called, she reminded herself yet again.

As she opened the door, he stepped in and threw his arms around her, swinging her off the floor as he hugged her. "I missed you. I wanted to come and see you at work today, but wasn't sure I could without doing this right there in the shop." He set her down and grinned. "And I know how much you would've hated that so I decided to wait." He swooped down and gave her a quick kiss. "So how was your weekend?" He took off his jacket hanging it on a hook in the closet, then strolled in and flopped down on the couch.

"My weekend was fine," she replied, thinking he was becoming a little too comfortable in her house. "How was yours?"

"Long." He patted the seat beside him. She walked over and sat in a chair across from him. He smiled, "I was afraid I was going to have to start over after leaving you alone all weekend. I was right, you're all prickly again. Luckily I don't discourage easily."

Her eyebrows rose. "Easily," she repeated. "So that means you can be discouraged, it's just difficult to do."

"That depends on how badly I want something, and whether I think it's going to be impossible in the long run." He held up his hand as she opened her mouth to speak. "I know what you're going to say and I don't happen to agree. I don't believe this is going to be impossible, just... challenging." Lowering his voice, he added, "I love a challenge."

They contemplated each other for a moment, then he said, "I'm hungry. Would you like to go out? Or we could order something and eat here."

Definitely too comfortable. "I was just getting ready to make a sandwich. If you're interested there's more than enough." She could usually speak her mind about anything, but it was hard for her to be out and out rude to anyone. She wasn't completely comfortable having him here, but she couldn't just throw him out either.

"That sounds great if it's not too much trouble."

"No trouble."

While they ate, he told her about his weekend. How the problem with the heat-treated parts was fixed, putting his house on the market, the standard red tape hassle of getting ones personal info and address changed. As usual the longer she was around him, the more relaxed she became. When everything was cleaned up, she stretched. She would love to take a walk. She did fairly often after supper. Behind her property was a wooded area belonging to a neighbor. They had assured her she was welcome to walk back there any time she wanted. A gorgeous sunset started to form. If she were alone she would walk along the trees and enjoy it. A sunset stroll to the woods with Drake brought up images she didn't need. She also knew if she asked he would take it as encouragement.

Drake watched her face as she watched the colors spread across the sky. He walked over to her and took her hand. "Come on, let's go outside." She eyed him skeptically. "I promise to behave." Startled, her eyes widened, and he laughed. "You can be fairly transparent sometimes." He dragged her over to the door, retrieving their jackets from the closet.

They walked along her usual path talking easily about how much they each liked the outdoors, places they had traveled, and where they grew up. Kate didn't say anything when Drake slid his hand into hers entwining their fingers. She continued to listen as he told her a story about his brother. Concentrating intently on his words kept her mind off the touch of his hand, the warmth she felt at being so close to him. They sat on an old log at the edge of the woods and watched the sunset. Kate shivered slightly and Drake removed his jacket, slipping it around her shoulders. She closed her eyes. It hadn't been the cool evening air that made her shiver, it had been the sensations he was creating inside her. Of course, she couldn't tell him that. The jacket still held the warmth of his body and the faint smell of his after-shave only made it worse.

Kate cleared her throat, "I think we should be getting back. It's going to be really dark soon, and it's easy to trip out here."

The walk back was quiet. She wished he would talk. Maybe tell her more stories about his family. The silence seemed to somehow create an intimacy between them she didn't want. He didn't come in when they reached the house. Instead he turned to face her. In a strained whisper, he explained. "I promised earlier to behave myself. If I'm going to keep that promise I'd better leave now." His breathing was ragged and his lashes lowered. He bent and kissed her gently on the forehead. "Sweet dreams, Kate." He released her and strode to his car.

His well-practiced message worked again. That night she dreamed of him, as she often did. Sometimes they were quiet contented dreams of the two of them spending time together laughing and enjoying each other's company. Other nights like tonight they were highly emotional dreams leaving her feeling drained and exposed. A couple of nights, she had incredibly intimate and intensely erotic dreams about him. It was always hard to face him after one of those, as if somehow he would look into her eyes and see the scenes her subconscious had played out.

Drake spent two more evenings at her house that week. They spent hours sitting in front of the fireplace talking. Friday came and Kate decided she needed to get away. She had a feeling if she didn't leave town she would somehow find herself spending most of the weekend with Drake. Not only was he getting too comfortable at her house, but she was getting too comfortable around him. Formulating a plan she called a cousin she hadn't seen in awhile. Relieved to find out Cheryl was free, Kate made arrangements to drive down right after work and stay until Sunday afternoon.

Kate was glad she called when she did because fifteen minutes after returning from lunch Drake called the cage. "Hi, Kate. I'd like to take you out this weekend. Would tonight or tomorrow night be better for you?"

"Actually neither. I'm going to be out of town all weekend."

"Running away from me, Kate?"

"No I'm not running away." *Hiding for a while possibly, but not running away.* "I'm spending the weekend with my cousin. We rarely get to see each other and as it happens she's free all weekend, so I'm going to go visit. You may not believe this, but there are parts of my life that don't involve you." *I intend to spend the weekend figuring out exactly which parts those are.*

"When will you be back?"

"Not until late Sunday night, and I'm leaving right after work. I hope you have a nice weekend." She hung up the phone before he could say anything else.

She rushed home after work, packed quickly, and was on her way to her cousin's house in record time. It took about three hours to make the trip. The farther from home she got, the more relaxed she became. That thought disturbed her. She loved her home and didn't like the fact someone made her feel the need to be away from it.

Kate felt great Monday morning. The weekend had been fun. She needed to make a point of seeing Cheryl more often. She thought she was ready for anything when she walked into work. How wrong she had been.

The shelves holding the fixtures were old and only housed four shelves per unit. New more efficient storage units had been ordered weeks ago and arrived today. Every fixture had to be removed while the old shelves were disassembled and new ones were set in place. Since this system was different, a new location had to be assigned to each fixture as it was put away.

Although paperwork for the location changes had been prepared in advance, and space had been cleared to set the fixtures while the shelves were changed, there was no way to lessen the amount of physical labor involved. Two people were sent over from another department to help, but it was still a grueling day.

Kate worked two extra hours that day and was about three-quarters of the way done. By the time she arrived home, she was exhausted and a bit stiff from all the lifting. Although handling the fixtures was part of her job, she wasn't used to moving almost all of them in one day. After thirty minutes of soaking in a hot bath, she was too tired to fix herself a meal, choosing instead to pass through the kitchen and flop on the couch in front of the TV.

*****

When Drake arrived carrying Chinese take out he knocked, but nobody answered. He tried the door and was surprised to find it unlocked. Knowing Kate didn't usually leave her house open. He went in figuring she just didn't hear the knock. As he put the food on the table he heard the TV and went to investigate. Having spent most of the day out on the shop floor he had noticed how hard her day had been, so he wasn't completely surprised to find her asleep.

After turning off the television, Drake sat on the coffee table and watched her. His heart constricted in his chest. She was the most incredible woman he had ever known. She had such power over him and didn't even seem to know it. He didn't understand the bizarre relationship they had, and no longer even cared to question it. If another woman had pushed him away half as much as this one had he would've walked away without a second glance. Somehow though, he felt Kate needed him. He couldn't explain how or why, somehow he just felt it. Something was pulling them together. Kate was fighting it, but he knew she felt it too. She just wasn't ready to give in to it yet. He would give her time, not enough space to get away from him, but enough time to accept what was to be between them. It was getting difficult though. He wanted her... in every way possible. He wanted to live in the same house with her. See her every morning, eat every meal with her, spend every evening with her, and have her in his arms every night. He wanted to know she was his, and only his.

He grimaced. He had never considered himself a jealous man, but even knowing she was not involved with any one at work, sharing her with so many men everyday, and watching her talk, laugh, and occasionally flirt with them nearly tore him apart. He had to stop himself each and every day from announcing to the entire company that she was his. He dropped his head and rubbed the back of his neck smiling a humorless smile knowing how much she would hate it if he followed through with an announcement like that.

Looking around the room, he remembered the food and went to the kitchen to stow it in the refrigerator. Returning to the living room, he looked again at Kate. She laid on the edge of the cushions with her head on a small pillow. He slowly eased in behind her, positioning himself between her and the back of the couch. She wriggled and started to lift her head. He shifted the pillow back so he could use it as he slid his arm beneath her head. With a gentle hand he lowered her head to his shoulder, then pulled the blanket down from behind him and spread it over her.

Kate stretched her arms and yawned his name. "Drake?"

He smiled, lightly massaging her arm and shoulder. "Yes."

Her eyelids fluttered, but she couldn't seem to keep them open. "You sure like to press an advantage, don't you?" Her voice was quiet and slightly slurred from sleep.

He chuckled. "Yes, I do."

She moaned softly, tilting her head a bit giving him better access to her shoulder. Kate yawned again as she snuggled back against him, then whispered drowsy and contented. "I'm going to be so mad at you later."

Drake chuckled again. Still massaging her tight muscles, he leaned forward and whispered, "I know, but I don't mind. You're positively adorable when you're angry."

He smiled when a barely discernible grin passed across her lips as she drifted back to sleep.

Chapter Six

Two hours later, Kate stretched and yawned. Drake tried not to laugh when she wrinkled her nose, then rubbed it with the back of her hand. He wondered if this was how she always woke up. If it was he didn't think he would ever get tired of watching her. He had dozed for a short time, but mostly just enjoyed being able to hold her. Her hair smelled of wildflowers and spilled over his shoulder. He would never get tired of that either. She yawned again then snuggled against him, moaning with the same contented sigh she had earlier. Her soft curves pressed into the length of his body. Yet another thing he would love to experience on a daily basis. His mind wandered to other things he would love to experience with her when suddenly her body tensed.

A smirk pulled at the corners of his mouth as he waited for her reaction to waking up in his arms. Her head tilted slowly as she looked down at the arm wrapped around her waist. She slowly lifted the blanket and peeked under it. She breathed a sigh of relief. "At least I'm dressed."

Drake laughed, "What did you expect? That I would strip you while you slept?"

"I wouldn't put anything past you at this point." She yawned again. "Actually, since living by myself I've picked up a few bad habits. Running around the house half dressed is one of them. As tired as I was when I came home I was afraid maybe I hadn't put anything on after my bath."

"I wouldn't have a problem with that," he whispered low in her ear. "If you're more comfortable in less clothing feel free to take off anything you like." She made a disgusted sound. "Really, I wouldn't want to be responsible for making you uncomfortable in your own home."

"Ha! That's never been a problem for you before." she retorted. Drake laughed again. He loved sparring with her.

He didn't want to get up, and noticed despite her grousing, she made no attempt to leave his arms either. It was because of that fact he knew he'd better move. If he stayed here much longer things could get out of hand fast. He wouldn't be content to lie here and simply talk. He wanted much more.

"I saw how hard you worked today. I wanted to come in and help you, but figured you'd bite my head off if I tried. So instead I brought you supper. If you're hungry we could get up and eat." He lowered his lips to her ear. "If not, then we could stay right here and find something more entertaining to do." He softly nibbled the back of her neck.

He felt her shiver slightly before she said, "Actually I'm starved!" and nearly leapt off the couch. "What did you bring?" Her voice was not quite as high this time.

Drake grinned. He had a feeling that would get her off the sofa. He knew she needed more time. He just hoped it wasn't much more. "I brought Chinese. I hope that's okay."

"Great, I love Chinese." Kate started for the kitchen.

After a good meal, some casual conversation, and a quick clean up, Drake decided it was time he left. He knew she was going to have another hard day tomorrow and didn't want to keep her up late. He pulled her into his arms and held her with his cheek resting on her hair. "Try not to work too hard tomorrow."

"It shouldn't be as bad as today. Most of it's done. I can take my time with the rest." She didn't return his hug, but didn't pull away from him either. He slowly rubbed her back then pressed her body tighter against his. Drake listened as her breathing become shallow and unsteady. Sliding his hand up to gently massage her neck and shoulder he could feel the pulse of her accelerated heart beat. Intense desire coursed through him in response. She may not have put her arms around him, but she couldn't stop her body's reaction to his touch. Drake tilted his head, and with a curled finger under her chin, lifted her lips to his. He felt her tremble slightly, her eyes closed and her lips softened as he caressed them with his own. He felt her subtle response to his kiss before she suddenly pulled away.

"I, um...better get some sleep. Goodnight." She spun on her heel and escaped down the hall.

Drake let himself out of the house making sure the door was locked and got into his car. Once inside he sat for a while, trying to regain his composure. She had started to kiss him. He felt it. He took a deep breath and smiled with renewed determination.

*****

The next day Kate was in a foul mood. Slamming parts around and trying not to throw things. She should've been almost done with the fixtures by now. Instead she wasn't much farther along than she had been when she started this morning. With all the mistakes she had made so far she might even be farther behind than she was when she arrived.

Kate sent the two men helping her to lunch. She leaned against a shelf in the back and took a deep breath. "You have got to get a grip." Turning, she spotted the soft cotton buffs stacked beside her. She reached over picked one up and slammed it against the post.

"Abusing the buffs again I see. Do you suppose there's a support group for that?"

Kate spun around and found Ray standing just behind her.

"If there is feel free to sign me up. I'm willing to try anything at this point."

Her supervisor gave her a gentle smile, "Is there anything I can do to help?"

Kate heaved a sigh and blinked back the tears threatening to spill. "No. It's time for lunch. I'll use the time to try and pull myself together as well as get something to eat."

"Okay, but if there's anything I can do, let me know."

Kate smiled, "Thanks, Ray. I really appreciate the offer."

"Anytime." He patted her shoulder and walked out. Kate took another deep breath and closed her eyes. *It was just a kiss. I was too tired to think straight. End of story. Now get over it and do your job.*

She hadn't been able to concentrate on anything all morning. Well, anything other than Drake and last night's kiss, that is. She had tried to stay indifferent to him and couldn't. She knew he had been trying to carefully entrench himself in her life. She just hadn't known how to stop it. Dropping her head into her hands, she whispered, "This wasn't supposed to happen." Last night she had been tired after a hard day. He had held her, kept her warm while she slept, fed her when she was hungry, and talked to her when she would've otherwise been lonely. She had been alone for so long. Other than Drake, she couldn't honestly remember the last time someone had hugged her.

Then there was that kiss. His kisses always stirred something in her, but last night she had wanted to kiss him back. Had started to kiss him back. Kate raised her head and took one more deep, calming breath. Even being as tired and vulnerable as she was she had stopped. She hadn't let it continue. She found some comfort in that and decided to make a renewed effort to get her job done as soon as she took a break.

As Kate entered the break room everyone went quiet. She noticed the men all looking at her.

"What?" she asked, as she glanced down to make sure everything was properly zipped and buttoned.

Terry was the first to speak. "We were just watching to see if your head was going to spin all the way around."

Kate knew she had been in a bad mood and had taken it out on people she shouldn't have. She looked at all the faces staring at her with guarded expressions, and couldn't help but smile. "That bad, huh?"

"Bad? I thought we were going to have to put poor Dave in therapy after his last trip to the cage."

Steve joined in. "We always thought they locked you in there to protect you from us. Now we know it was actually to protect us from you. We've all been trying to send Smitty for our tools today, but even he wouldn't go. He said you had too many sharp objects in there."

Kate bought a soda from the machine and sat down. The two men she sat between scooted away from her. A laugh escaped her and she shook her head. "I've been dealing with your foul moods for years. There's not one of you that hasn't come to the window and cussed or yelled at one time or another. Bad days, broken tooling, program errors, cars that don't run, relationship problems, the list goes on and I've heard it all. So if I have a bad day now and then the least you guys can do is return the favor and deal with it."

"Well now. You bring up a good point," Terry said. "We share with you, so there's no reason you can't share with us."

Kate looked skeptical. "What do you mean?"

"I mean obviously something has you all riled up. I'm guessing it's the flower guy. So who is he and what'd he do?"

"I'm just having a bad day. Everybody does once in a while. Today is just my turn. In case you haven't noticed I have an unusual workload this week and I'm tired." Kate stood up, "I'd better get back. It may take me a while to find the guys who were helping me. They're probably hiding from me by now."

She did manage to do better the second half of the day. She apologized to her helpers and made a point to be extra nice to them until they were done.

That evening she went home, took a quick shower, and packed a change of clothes in her overnight bag. She arrived at Sue's a short time later.

"Hi, I need a place to crash tonight. Do you have any plans for this evening?"

"I have a date, but I could cancel," replied Sue surprised.

"No, don't cancel. I'm exhausted and just want a quiet place to be until tomorrow morning."

"You live alone outside of town with no close neighbors. Why would you come to my apartment in town for a quiet place to be?"

"Lets just say my house isn't as quiet as it used to be." Kate walked over and plopped down on the couch. "Will I be in the way? I can go out to eat if you and your date were going to stay in tonight. Or you could use my place."

"No, we were going out. I have to work in the morning so we weren't planning to be late. He'll be here in about twenty minutes and I should be back by nine or so. Are you sure you don't want me to cancel? Do you need to talk?"

"No. I'm tired of talking. The time alone will be nice. You go and enjoy your date."

Kate managed to avoid Drake over the next two days. It gave her a chance to regroup and convince herself she had blown things out of proportion where Drake was concerned.

Friday at lunchtime the phone rang. "Hi, Kate. Are you going to run off somewhere this weekend?"

"No, I have too much to do this weekend to be able to get away." She hoped he would take the hint, but wasn't surprised when he didn't.

"I'm glad you'll be around. I haven't seen you much lately." There was accusation in his voice.

"I've been busy."

"Busy avoiding me?" Was that humor she heard in his tone now? "You can't do that forever though. If you don't agree to go out with me I may be forced to camp on your doorstep. I have a tent, and I'm not afraid to use it."

It irritated her he could rouse her sense of humor so easily. She couldn't stay mad at someone she found amusing. Also, she would never convince him she wasn't interested if she kept letting him draw her into these teasing and sometimes flirtatious conversations.

"Just because you haven't seen me, doesn't mean I've been avoiding you. It simply means I don't feel the need to pencil you in on my list of things to do." She tried to sound stern, but got the feeling she didn't come across that way when the sound of his laughter echoed through the phone.

She was glad he couldn't see her face when his voice dropped into that tone that always seemed to flow over her and caress her nerve endings. "I want to see you this weekend, Kate. We can go to dinner and a movie, or we can spend the evening at your house. We could go to my apartment if you like. I could show you where I live. That way you could come and visit me whenever you like."

"Gee, it all sounds so great I just can't make up my mind. Tell you what, I'll think about it and get back to you. Now I have to get to lunch before my break is over. Bye."

Kate hung up and grabbed her purse. When she had her lunch and sat down at her usual table, everybody stared at her. "Now what?"

"You were talking to the flower guy just now, weren't you?" Terry accused.

"Don't you people have anything better to do than spy on me? What makes you think it was the flower guy?"

"Because you get all girlie when he's on the phone," Steve said. "And now we know."

"Know what?" she asked with a casualness she didn't feel.

"We know it's someone in the building. Someone who works here."

"What are you talking about?" Kate asked, getting more nervous by the minute.

"The phone call was an inside call. I was walking by the cage when it rang." His eyes narrowed." Two short rings."

"You guys sure jump to a lot of conclusions," she said, taking a bite of her sandwich.

"Come on, give. Who is he?" Steve asked.

Kate didn't answer, just took another bite of her sandwich, dabbing her mouth with a napkin.

Steve, who loves drama, stood up acting like a character out of an old black and white mystery. He squinted one eye and looked around the table, then in some unrecognizable foreign accent said, "We know it is someone in this building. Someone we all know. It could be someone in this very room. How do we know he isn't sitting at this very table?" He sat back down and again looked at each man.

Terry threw his hands in the air. "Okay, I confess! It's me!"

Kate laughed so hard her sides ached. As the laughing subsided, she reached over and patted Terry's rounded stomach, "As long as we're confessing we might as well tell them the rest. He's expecting my child."

This time everyone else at the table laughed until they hurt. Except Terry who was trying his best to look offended.

"No, it's not Terry," Kate said.

"Why not? What's wrong with me?"

"I just wouldn't have the conscience for it. You often talk about all the women who chase you. I would feel too guilty about taking you away from all of them."

"Okay," Steve said. "It's not Terry. We're weeding out suspects."

"What about me?" Ron asked.

"You mean other than the fact you're married?" Kate questioned.

"If you consider that a problem, then I guess that rules out Dennis and Paul here, too."

Steve spoke up again. Kate wasn't sure whether he was trying to sound French or German. "Good, good. Now we're getting somewhere. What about Smitty?"

Kate looked at Smitty and grinned. He was wriggling his eyebrows and flexing the muscles in his chest. Kate heaved a deep dramatic sigh. "I have to admit Smitty does give a girl something to think about. Unfortunately I just don't think I could get past the tattoos. Sorry, Smitty." She often teased him about his tattoos.

Steve looked past Kate, "What about Drake?"

Kate turned and found Drake standing a few feet from her.

He looked directly at her. "Yes, Kate, what about me?"

This game suddenly wasn't so fun. She refused, however, to give these guys any hint he was the flower guy. She eyed him for a moment. "I don't think so. He's too... I don't know, VP-ish."

"VP-ish?" Drake asked.

"Yeah, you know, big office, starchy dress shirts. Preppy." She gave him an apologetic look. "Basically not my type at all."

"Come on, Kate, the guy has to dress that way for his job," Dave said. "It isn't fair to judge a guy on how he dresses for work."

"Yeah," added Terry, "He's probably not so preppy outside of work." The other guys at the table nodded and agreed.

Kate couldn't believe they were all defending him. She looked around the table and stated, "Have you seen what he drives?"

Whistles, nods, and various sounds of understanding came from around the table. Steve looked at Drake sympathetically, "She's gotcha there, dude. You don't get much more preppy than that."

Drake grinned. "The car's not mine. A week before I left Indy some kid was showing off in his new sports car and totaled mine while it was parked. Bill rented this one for me until I can replace mine. So far I haven't had much time to car shop." He smiled at Kate. "So what kind of car do you see me in that isn't too preppy for you?"

"Hmm." Kate put her finger on her chin and squinted. "Possibly a small SUV."

He contemplated her a moment. "What do you drive?"

She realized her car was always in the garage, he probably hadn't ever seen it when he was over. "Us working girls can't afford fancy new cars. I drive a really old car."

Gasps and shrieks of outrage erupted around her.

Steve grabbed his chest. "Blaspheme! How dare you call it that."

Terry groaned with his head down on the table. "I can't believe she said that."

Drake's brow furrowed at the odd display. "What does she drive?"

Dave ignored the glare Kate gave him and looked at Drake. "She drives the one car in the parking lot we've all tried to get our hands on at one time or another. It's an all original nineteen sixty-six Mustang convertible."

Drake's eyes widened. "The blue one? I've seen it in the parking lot." He looked at Kate. "That's your car?"

"Yes." The buzzer rang signaling lunch was over and they all cleared their things and went back to work.

Kate was a bit jumpy the rest of the afternoon. She hadn't given Drake an answer about plans for the weekend and didn't think he would just forget about it. She didn't know if he would come to the cage, or he would wait and show up at her house.

She had considered spending the weekend with Sue or Missy, but didn't want to have to explain her actions. Sue still wondered about the other night. She could simply lock herself in the house and pretend she wasn't home if he came. That seemed too childish. She should just tell him once and for all she didn't want to see him anymore and be done with it. Although she had been fairly blunt about that before, and he hadn't ever listened.

The workday finally ended with no sign of Drake. Kate went home and changed into an old tee shirt and shorts intending to do her usual Friday night housework.

Part way through, the doorbell rang. It had to be Drake, her friends always just walked in. She found it strange she hadn't seen much of them lately. She knew she looked a mess. Her braid had come partially loose, her clothes were old, and she probably had dust all over her. She thought about ducking into the laundry room and pulling something better out of the dryer, then decided he would simply have to deal with her the way she was if he insisted on popping in at all hours. She walked over and pulled the door open. "What?"

"Well, hello to you too," Drake replied. "Can I come in?"

"I really am busy. I don't have time to socialize this evening." She didn't move.

"What are you doing? Is it something I can help you with?"

"Thanks for the offer, but no. I'm cleaning house."

"How long will it take?"

"I don't know I've let things go lately, so it will probably take a long time."

"I have to take care of a few things myself this evening, so I'll go do that and be back here in about two hours. That will give you time to work, then we can spend the rest of the evening together."

Kate squared her shoulders and glared at him. "You are the pushiest person I've every met. Why won't you take the hint and leave me alone?"

"Because I enjoy your company. I also know you enjoy mine when you let yourself relax." He leaned toward her again and his voice lowered. "We have something special, Kate, and I'm not willing to give up on it. I don't know exactly what you're afraid of, but I'm willing to stick around as long as it takes for you to get past it." He dropped a quick kiss on her cheek and said, "I'll be back in two hours."

Kate watched as he walked to his car. Slowly she closed the door and leaned against it. What was she going to do? She let out a scream of irritation, then got back to work. It was amazing how much work one could do when they were angry. She nearly scrubbed the pattern off the floor by the time she was done.

Twenty minutes before Drake was due back she took a shower and put on clean clothes. The doorbell rang as she entered the kitchen. She pulled the door open and stepped back for him to enter.

Drake had brought movies and they decided to eat in front of the TV again. After they finished, he covered the pizza and stacked the plates. When he stood, Kate assumed he was going to the kitchen. Instead he scooped her up and flopped her onto the couch. He slid behind her as he had done when he found her sleeping and pulled her back against him. "This is much better than sitting on the floor." Just as before, he took the blanket from the back of the couch and tossed it over of them.

She should be outraged. She should leap off the couch and tell him exactly what she thought of him.

A Dream to be Loved

She didn't think that would have the desired affect, however, considering at the moment she thought he was really warm, with strong comforting arms, and a broad solid chest.

Stop it! Stop it! Stop it! Her mind screamed. You have got to stop thinking about him like that. Drake pulled her closer and wrapped both arms around her. Kate was tense while she tried to decide whether she should do the safe thing and get up, or take a chance and enjoy being in his arms.

Before she could make up her mind he leaned close to her ear and whispered, "Just let me hold you, Kate." He kissed the back of her neck, then rested his head back down on the pillow.

Kate closed her eyes and concentrated on keeping her breathing steady. She really did want to stay where she was. Maybe it would be okay for a little while. Just this once.

When the movie was over, she slid off the couch and went to get another drink. She was standing at the sink when Drake walked up behind her. She turned, looking up at him. His eyes were dark and shadowed. She hadn't bothered to turn on a light when she came in. The only light in the room was from a small nightlight she always left on.

"Do you want another drink?" Her voice was a bit shaky. He was very close, and from the look in his eyes it wasn't a drink he wanted.

"No, I don't. I think we need to talk."

She ran her tongue across her dry lips, regretting it when she noticed how intently he watched the small nervous gesture.

"About what?"

"About us." He raised a finger to her lips when she would have protested. "Yes, there is an us whether you want to admit it or not. I think some things about our relationship need to change."

"Like what?" she asked hesitantly.

"Like kissing for instance. I don't think I should kiss you."

How odd that relief could so easily disguise itself as disappointment.

"Okay," she whispered.

Drake moved a step closer, lowering his voice. "I think instead, we should kiss each other." Moving closer yet, he slipped his hands around her waist.

Kate's hands tightened their grip on the edge of the counter as she leaned back a little farther, "Drake, I don't... I mean, we..."

As Drake started to lean toward her they heard, "Good grief, Kate," from Sue who had just come in. "You'll have to excuse her, Drake. She's normally a very intelligent woman, capable of dealing with highly complicated and technical situations. Unfortunately it's the simple concepts she sometimes has trouble with." Sue stopped directly behind Drake reaching around him to pry Kate's hands from the counter top. "It's like this dear." She pulled Kate's arms up and wound them around

Drake's shoulders. "That's much better," she said stepping back. "I came to get my other purse out of my room. I'll just grab it and be out of your way." Sue was down the hall and back in a flash. "You two have fun. I'll see you later."

When she was gone, Drake smiled. "I like your friends."

"Good. You can have that one."

Drake lowered his head and kissed her cheek. Then slowly kissed and nibbled his way to her ear and down the side of her neck. He gently pulled the tie from her hair, letting it spill across her shoulders and down her back. Winding his hand into the thick silky mass, he drew her head back allowing him room to explore the smooth sensitive skin at the base of her neck and under her chin. As he pulled her closer she whimpered softly, breathless and trembling in his arms, her fingers curled tight, each clenching a fistful of his shirt.

Don't kiss him, don't kiss him, don't kiss him.

She tried to concentrate as his lips trailed back toward hers. Then he whispered, "Kiss me, Kate. Don't think about it, don't fight it, just feel what's between us and kiss me." His words were husky and full of raw emotion, weakening Kate's reserve.

Maybe just this once. To see what it would be like to really kiss him. Just this once, just this, just this....

Kate had expected a hard passionate kiss. Instead Drake kissed her softly with such tenderness tears welled up in her eyes. Never before had she reacted to a kiss this way. She hadn't realized a simple physical act could be filled with such strong emotion. Unclenching her fists, she ran her fingers into his hair pulling him closer. The kiss deepened and a low sensual growl escaped him, sending ripples of pleasure spiraling through her body. She pressed against him as the kiss became more intense and demanding. Kate was completely lost to everything but Drake.

When he dragged his lips from hers, they were both shaking and gasping for breath. He pulled back slightly to look at her, then gently wiped away the tear that had spilled down her cheek. "Are you okay?"

"I think so." Her smile was uncertain and her words strained. "That was just... I wasn't expecting..."

Drake pulled her close. Settling her head on his shoulder, he whispered, "I know, I think it took us both by surprise."

*****

Drake was trembling as well, his emotions threatening to engulf him completely. He couldn't remember ever wanting to tell a woman he loved her before, but now, he was struggling to keep from it. He fought against it knowing she wasn't ready to hear it yet, but he would tell her soon.

Chapter Seven

Kate lay face down with her head under her pillow the next morning trying to block out memories. She had tossed and turned most of the night not being able to get Drake out of her head long enough to sleep. When she had drifted off, she dreamed about him. She never would have guessed a person with so little actual experience at something could dream in such graphic detail. Why was her subconscious torturing her this way? And why was her body so eager to help?

Drake had left shortly after kissing her the night before. He had held her for a few minutes, then gave her a soft goodnight kiss, bid her sweet dreams and left. "Sweet dreams, yeah right," she mumbled from under her pillow. Deciding she needed to get up and find something to take her mind off the man, she rolled out of bed.

It was shortly after ten when Kate came dragging into the kitchen. "You sure have taken to sleeping late on the weekends," Missy said.

"Even as late as it is, she looks like she could use a few more hours sleep," Sue added. "You look terrible. Long night?" she asked with a grin.

"Are you okay?" Missy asked. "You do look a little stressed."

"I'm fine, I just need some tea."

"So how did things go after I left last night?" Sue asked.

Kate turned and looked at the other two at the table. "Either of you want any tea?"

"I'd like some," said Kelsie. Missy shook her head no.

Kate went about her business.

"Well?" Sue said. "Are you going to tell us what happened?"

Kate looked at Missy and then Kelsie as she set a cup of tea in front of her. "I'm hungry, you didn't happen to bring anything for breakfast, did you?"

"Muffins," Kelsie answered, "They're beside the refrigerator."

"That sounds great." Kate grabbed the bag and her tea on the way to the table.

"Well?" Sue demanded, louder this time.

Kate looked at Missy. "I'll warn you now I'm not speaking to her. That way you can decide if you want to stay or not. We all know how obnoxious she can be when she's ignored.

Sue let out an exasperated breath. "Oh, come on. I was just helping you out."

Kate looked at Kelsie. "These muffins are really good. Did you make them or get them from that new bakery in town?"

They discussed the muffins, the new bakery, two other new stores that had just opened, and a few other things. Missy finally broke in, and said, "We came over to see if you had any plans for today. Your birthday is next Saturday, and we've decided what we want to do."

For as long as they had been friends, birthdays had always been treated special between them. They didn't try to do it bigger and better every year, simply different than what had been done before. They had made a vow as teens no matter what the rest of their lives were like to never get stuck in a rut when it came to celebrating birthdays.

To help keep that from happening it was also the tradition the three who weren't having the birthday got to choose the activity. That kept it interesting.

Kate couldn't believe she had actually forgotten it was time for her birthday. She took a deep breath. "So what's it going to be this year?"

"Something you would never come up with on your own," Kelsie smiled.

Missy continued, "We are going to go shopping and buy new evening wear so next weekend we can all go to that fancy new restaurant in Fort Wayne."

Kate nearly choked on her tea. "Evening wear? I hope you're talking about flannel pajamas for a restaurant hosting a theme party."

Kelsie laughed. "Of course not. It won't hurt you to dress up once in your life."

"I have dressed up. I have a dress in my closet."

"Yes, but it's as old as your car and would probably crumble from dry rot if you tried to take it off the hanger."

Kate gaped at her. Kelsie rarely spoke to anyone like that. She was always the quiet one. Surprisingly, she was the one Kate usually went to when she had a serious problem. Most people had the impression she was closest to Sue. In reality, her and Sue had lots of fun together and were good friends, but their basic values varied drastically when it came to personal issues.

"It's our decision," said Missy, "This is what we've decided. We can shop tomorrow or later in the week if you have plans today, but we are going."

Kate sighed, resigning herself to the fact it was going to happen. "I don't have any plans so we might as well go get this over with." She stood up and took her cup to the sink. "I'll go get dressed."

Kate arrived home five hours later loaded down with packages. Tossing them all on her bed, she couldn't believe she had bought so many clothes today. It wasn't the money that bothered her, she could afford it. What amazed her was she had just bought more clothes in one trip than she would normally buy in a two year span. She didn't shop often. Her friends teased her about being a penny pincher sometimes, but it wasn't like that. She simply didn't need much. After her bills were paid and she pocketed some cash to put gas in her car and the vending machines at work, everything else went into the bank. She didn't have a vast amount left over each week but it had added up over the past few years.

Her job was not conducive to an expensive wardrobe considering she came home stained with oil and machine coolant most days. So why did many of these bags contain sweaters, blouses, and pants that were not standard denim? Not to mention that slinky little black thing the girls made her buy. She groaned and flopped down on the bed. If they thought she was wearing it, and that contraption that went under it, out in public they had another thing coming.

Kate couldn't help but grin thinking about what the guys at work would say if they saw her in a slinky black dress. They would probably never stop laughing at her. She started to wonder what Drake would think about it, but slammed that thought shut before it could fully form. She wouldn't find it funny if Drake thought she looked silly in it. "It's not like he'll ever get the chance to see you in it anyway," she said out loud.

She hopped off the bed and dug through the packages. Deciding it was silly to have bought so many clothes she probably would never wear. She picked out a few pieces she especially liked and bagged the rest to take back Monday.

The dress she would like to take back, but knew according to birthday law she would have to wear it Saturday night. She hung it in the closet, then opened the little bag that came with it. Slowly she pulled the black silk teddy out and looked at it. "What were you thinking?" She groaned as she slid her fingers down garter straps that were attached and wrinkled her nose. "Like I would even know how to get into something like this."

Running a hand across the silk she had to admit it felt nice but wasn't sure she would feel comfortable having it on. It just wasn't the kind of thing she ever wore. "It's not like they'll know if I have it on or not." The deal had been they all bought new sexy dresses and matching underclothes with garters and silk stockings. Sue had gone for an outrageous sheer lace bustier with matching garter all the same dark red as her dress. Missy had chosen a jade dress with matching bra, panty, and garter set. Kelsie like herself had gone simple and black. "Everybody needs a little black dress," she said, repeating what Kelsie had told her.

Kate finished putting away what she planned to keep and set the rest on a chair by the door as she headed for the kitchen checking the time. She and Kelsie were going to a movie later. Drake wouldn't be by. He had told her last night he was going to be busy all weekend. Kate was glad. She needed time to sort out what had happened to her last night.

Maybe she should talk to Kelsie about it. Discussing it with someone might help her see the situation more clearly. Possibly help her find a way to discourage Drake before he had a chance to hurt her too badly.

With that decided she pulled a soda out of the refrigerator. Going back to the bedroom she retrieved her sketchpad and pencils out of the closet and went to the living room. Drawing usually helped her relax. She would just have to make sure she drew something other than Drake's face. She flipped open the pad and looked through some of her drawings. When she got to Drake's picture, she stared at it. There was still something about it that bothered her, but she couldn't yet figure out what. She moved past it and found a blank page.

She was still drawing when Kelsie came in. While Kate found her shoes, Kelsie picked up the sketchpad and flipped through it. "I haven't seen you draw in years. What made you pick it back up?"

"I don't know. I was cleaning a while back and ran across that in a closet. I guess I decided to see if I was still capable. Once I started, I realized how much I missed it." Kate turned and saw the astonished look on Kelsie's face.

"Not only have you not lost your ability, I'd say you've gotten better. Or is it simply a particular subject matter that inspires you to this level of ability?" Kelsie turned the tablet around and Kate saw Drake's face.

"I, um, I'm not sure how that happened. It just sort of showed up on the paper."

"Wow. I knew you two were seeing quite a bit of each other, but I didn't realize it was this serious."

"It's just a sketch," Kate said. "It's not serious."

"My dear, nobody could mistake the way you feel about him after seeing this."

"What do you mean?" Kate asked defensively.

"I mean, look at it. This is not a simple sketch. I'm no art expert, but I can see the emotion in this. There's no way you could have put that look in his eyes unless you've seen it there, and no way you could have recreated it so accurately unless you felt it to some extent yourself. I know you, Kate. I've seen your other drawings. I know you need a model of some kind to do your best work. Unless Drake posed for this, you created it from memory. If that's the case, then you would have to feel pretty strongly about him to do this. The way you painstakingly detailed every feature of his face shows how much you care."

That's when Kate saw it. The thing she knew was there but couldn't quite grasp. Kelsie was right, her feelings were on that page. Her feelings for Drake. She hadn't wanted to see it. The drawing had been her way of expressing it without having to face reality.

Kate dropped her head in her hands and started to cry as she sank into a chair.

Kelsie came over and hugged her. "I knew this would happen someday. I only hoped you'd be ready for it when it did."

"Well, I'm not," she cried. "I can't believe I let this happen." She took a deep breath and wiped her eyes. "I'll just have to get over it. It'll take awhile, but I can do it."

"Why do you have to get over it? Drake is a really great guy."

Kate laughed, though not really amused. "Yes he is. That's just it, he's a Vice President. Obviously, he's looking for someone to fool around with until a proper wife can be found. I work in a machine shop, he can't really be serious about me. He's new in town, he just hasn't met anybody else here yet. In time he'll lose interest." Kate hoped Kelsie would accept that as the reason. The real reason she couldn't get involved was too humiliating.

"I haven't gotten that impression from him. Has he tried to pressure you into sleeping with him?"

"No."

"Then obviously he's interested in something more. He's a man who happens to have a title attached to his job. So what? I don't understand why you think he wouldn't be interested in you. He'd be lucky to have you, and I think he knows that. Why don't you give him a chance?"

"There are a lot of things I'm willing to chance, but walking into a relationship that's doomed from the beginning is not one of them." Kate wiped her eyes again and stood up. "If we don't leave soon, we'll miss our movie."

"We don't have to see a movie, if you'd rather, we can stay here," Kelsie offered.

"No, I need to get out for awhile. I've been feeling a bit claustrophobic lately."

*****

Even though it had gone fairly well for a Monday, Kate was glad work was over. She hadn't been getting much sleep lately. She had never been one to take naps unless she was sick, but recently found she wanted one often. She had to get a grip on this Drake thing. She hadn't seen him all weekend and should've been glad. Instead she had constantly wondered what he was doing. He told her he would be busy but he hadn't said at what.

That evening like clockwork Drake showed up at suppertime. "Hello. Are we eating in or out this evening?"

Kate glared at him, not moving away from the door. "Don't you have a home of your own?"

"Yes, I do, but I like it here better. Now, I'm guessing either you're not moving because you don't want to let me in, or your waiting for a hello kiss. I'm going to go with the latter." In one smooth motion he stepped to her, slid his hands around her waist, and lowered his head. Her breath caught in her throat as his lips touched hers. This kiss was different than the last one. It didn't begin slow and soft. It started out hard and passionate, leaving no room for rational thought.

By the time Drake lifted his head, Kate didn't think she could stand on her own. Her legs were shaky and she was out of breath. Her arms were wound tightly around his neck. Drake scooped her up and stepped inside kicking the door shut. He carried her into the living room and dropped down on the sofa with her on his lap. "Much better," he murmured as he kissed her again.

Kate couldn't believe what was happening to her. It's not like she had never been kissed before. Men she'd gone out with had kissed her. She usually enjoyed it. Found it quite nice at times in fact, but not one of them had ever affected her like this.

Her mind seemed to have no control over her body. His kiss was demanding. He took and demanded she give... and she did, willingly. What shocked her more, however, was what happened next. Drake started to release her and Kate tightened her grip on him, running a hand into his hair. Now she took and demanded he give... and he did, without reservation. She would have never thought herself capable of such things. It inflamed her even more to realize she had the same affect on him he had on her. As she kissed him, she felt his heart beat even faster against her hand, his breathing became heavier and he sighed with a moan of unrestrained desire.

This time she was the one to release him, slowly pulling her hand from his hair as she looked into those dark hooded eyes. "Drake, I...." She didn't know what to say.

"It's okay, sweetheart, you don't have to say anything." He ran a hand down her back. Tugging her forward as he kissed her neck. Drawing away, he whispered, "Oh, Kate. If kissing is like this between us, can you imagine what it's going to be like when we finally make lo..."

Kate's hand clamped over his mouth before he could finish, then scrambled off his lap and to the kitchen. When she heard him coming she ran down the hall to her bathroom. She looked at her reflection in the mirror as she tried to catch her breath. Her eyes were dark and her lips were red and swollen. Her cheeks carried a light flush. She quickly splashed cold water on her face and dabbed it with a towel. She knew she was being ridiculous and over reacting, but she couldn't help it. He had almost said the unthinkable out loud. She had dreamed about it happening many times, but rationalized that one couldn't help what the subconscious did during sleep. She had been careful not to let such thoughts enter her conscious mind. Looking at herself again, she realized he had said when not if. He seemed sure it was going to happen. Of course, she hadn't done anything recently to give him reason to believe the contrary.

Splashing her face one more time with cold water, she hoped to revive her ability to think rationally. Looking herself right in the eye she said, "You're a grown woman. Start acting like one and stop over reacting. People kiss all the time, it's no big deal." Kate decided it was probably some hormonal change her body was going through causing her to have such a strong physical reaction. After all, weren't women her age supposed to have physical needs? That had to be all it was. She hoped that was it at least, because she was running out of explanations and excuses.

After folding the towel and carefully placing it back on the rack, she smoothed down her clothes, squared her shoulders, and went to the kitchen. She pulled shaved ham and cheese slices out of the refrigerator. As she was getting the bread, Drake walked into the room.

"I'm going to have a sandwich, do you want one?" she asked, her voice devoid of emotion.

"Yes. That will satisfy one of my appetites."

Kate bit back a retort and continued making the sandwiches. Drake strolled over behind her and slid his hands around her waist. "How long are you going to pretend this isn't happening?" he asked, kissing the back of her neck. "You're going to have to acknowledge it sooner or later." He tightened his arms around her, pulling her tight against him.

Kate's hands started to tremble as she finished her task.

"I'm not going away, Kate. Not only am I not going away, but I'm also getting tired of feeling like I'm sneaking around. I'm not ashamed of my feelings for you, and I want people to know you're mine. I know that may sound archaic or chauvinistic, but it's how I feel." His voice carried a tinge of frustration. "Do you have any idea what it's like for me to see you with all those men everyday?" He sighed against her neck. "It's all I can do some days not to stand out there and chase them away from you. I want to tell each and every one of them you're mine and they can't have you." He let out a rough self-mocking laugh. "The only thing stopping me so far is the fact you're locked safely behind the fence and they can't get to you. I can't promise it will stop me much longer."

"First of all," Kate replied sternly. "I'm not with all those men, I simply work there and dealing with them is my job. I consider many of them friends, but that's all. Second," her voice started to falter. "I'm not yours, and we're not sneaking around. I'm staying home and you keep showing up, that's not sneaking around. If you don't like the way I do things you, don't have to keep coming over." Her whole body trembled now as she fought back tears.

"Yes, I do have to come over. Until I can convince you to see me other places I will continue to be here." He reached out and took the sandwiches. Kate followed him to the table. As they ate she watched him, trying to figure out why he was doing this to her. She couldn't possibly have anything he would want. He was terrific. He held a position few men his age had achieved. He was intelligent, gorgeous, she assumed reasonably wealthy, so what was he doing here? He could have his pick of women, why was he wasting time with the one nobody wanted?

She was considering asking him that question point blank when Sue walked in. Relief washed over her at not having to be alone with him anymore this evening and let the subject drop.

Chapter Eight

Wednesday after work, Kate walked behind Smitty on the way out the door, digging through her purse for her keys. Not noticing he'd stopped, she ran into him. "Smitty! What are you doing? I almost broke my nose." She looked around and saw many of the guys standing along the sidewalk and at the edge of the parking lot. She leaned sideways and peeked around Smitty. Drake stood propped against a brand new SUV. He looked directly at her and said, "You can drive mine if I can drive yours." Laughter rumbled all around her.

"No thanks. I'll just stick with mine," she said nervously. Hoping nobody would read too much into this. Looking at him though, she got the impression he had other ideas. An uneasy feeling dropped into the pit of her stomach, then crept up her spine. Smitty glanced down at her when she absently grabbed the back of his shirt.

"You can at least go for a ride with me. After all, you're the one who thought I should get an SUV. I'd like to see if this meets with your approval."

"You're capable of figuring out what you want without my help."

"Okay if not a drive, how about dinner?"

"It's too bad, Drake, but you're a few weeks too late," Steve said. "In all the years she's worked here we've never known her to have a boyfriend until recently. Now it would seem she's taken."

"I know she is," replied Drake meaningfully.

"Well thanks for the offer, but I'm really not interested," she responded quickly, hoping to end this without too much speculation.

Drake's eyes challenged her. Crossing his arms over his chest and one ankle over the other, he said, "That's not the impression I got the other night when we were kissing."

Kate felt as though the ground dropped out from under her. She could neither breathe nor move. Although she didn't look around she knew every eye in the parking lot was on her.

"Dang! You're the flower guy?" asked Steve. Kate heard low whistles and murmuring all around.

"I send her flowers, take her out to a nice restaurant, even buy the vehicle she recommends. We spend the evenings at her house snuggling on her couch, she kisses me like it's forever, then casually tells me in front of the whole shop she's not interested." Drake shook his head. "And women complain about the way men treat them."

"I..." Kate glanced up and saw everyone glaring at her. "That's not exactly what happened," she said defensively.

"Don't you guys think she should come with me so we can talk about this?" asked Drake, looking around for support. "I think I deserve an explanation."

There was a resounding "Yes" from all around her. Smitty looked at her with obvious disapproval. "Smitty, I..."

"I'm not the one you need to explain to." Shocking everyone, he turned and swept her off the ground. Drake opened the passenger door as Smitty reached the curb. She was unceremoniously dropped into the seat and the door shut beside her. Drake stuck out his hand, "Thanks, Smitty."

Smitty shook his hand. "No problem. Good luck."

Drake grinned, "Thanks."

Murder is illegal, murder is illegal, murder is illegal. Although she tried, Kate couldn't think of a reason not to do him bodily harm. He climbed into the driver's seat and they pulled out of the parking lot.

"Well, I'm about to learn two new things about you," Drake said.

"What things?" she ground out.

"Just how much of a temper you have, and how long you can hold a grudge."

"Not to mention my penchant for revenge," she mumbled.

He chuckled. "At least you're not giving me the silent treatment."

She sat there steaming. "Oh, I wouldn't be too glad just yet. I have a feeling it won't be long and you'll be sorry I'm still speaking to you."

Drake reached over and took her hand. "Is this going to be our first official fight?"

"You..." She jerked her hand away and let out an exasperated sound, like a scream, but not as loud. "You are the most infuriating man I have ever met. And that is no small feat considering how many I've met. You are arrogant and pushy, you assume way too much, and you don't listen to a thing anybody else has to say. You don't seem to care how difficult you have just made my life. I've tried to be nice because you're a friend of Bill's and Vice President of the company I work for, but as of this moment, I don't care who you are or what you do..."

"Finally!"

"What is that supposed to mean?"

"I mean I've been trying to find a way to get you to see past my title. That's what Vice President is, the title of my job. It's what I do, not who I am." He raked his fingers through his hair. "Most of the women I dated before only wanted to go out with me for what I did, not who I was. So it's ironic when I finally find a woman I want to be with more than any other, she won't go out with me because of what I do. Have you ever taken the time to see who I am? I know when you get your mind off work, you find my company enjoyable, and me attractive."

Kate felt some of the wind leave her sails. "Look, it doesn't matter. I'm not interested in a relationship. I like living by myself. Trust me

A Dream to be Loved

when I say I wouldn't make a good girlfriend. As a matter of fact, I'm surprised you haven't come to that conclusion already. You don't seem to grasp the obvious very easily."

"On the contrary, I think it's you who is missing the obvious. If you would stop fighting your feelings, you'd see we have something very special. It's a very natural thing. I don't understand why you are working so hard to complicate it."

"I like my life just the way it is. Or was, before you threw it into chaos."

"Everybody needs to be shaken up a little now and then. I know you threw me for a loop the day I met you." He took her hand again and brought it to his lips. It took great effort not to react when his lips caressed her skin.

"Now that you have humiliated me in front of my coworkers, can I go home?"

"No. We can go to my place so I can change, then I'll take you out to dinner. Any place special you want to go?"

"Other than home? No."

They pulled into a small parking lot behind an apartment building downtown. Drake came around the truck as she got out.

"Remember, I didn't pick this out. It's just until... I find someplace more suitable." With a hand at the small of her back, he let her into the apartment. "I'll just be a few minutes, make yourself comfortable."

As Drake made his way to the small bedroom at the back he said a little prayer he hadn't blown it today. He knew he had taken a big chance. He had gained some respect in the shop and most of the guys liked him, but he didn't have the relationship with them Kate did. He hoped by making such a public display earlier it would show them how serious he was about her and she could get past worrying about rumors. It was obvious people knew her well enough to know she wasn't a floozy, or someone who would try to gain favors by dating a VP. He didn't think she would believe it until she saw it for herself though. Then that would be one less hurdle in their way. He was determined to start removing her excuses one by one until she had none left and had to acknowledge that they belonged together.

He had nearly just blown it a few minutes ago with that comment about the apartment. When he first came to town his plan was to find a house. Now, however, he decided to wait until they could decide together where they wanted to live. He knew he was being very optimistic, but he couldn't stop thinking about what it would be like to live in the same house with Kate. He was getting impatient.

*****

While she waited, Kate wandered around the room. It was a very nice apartment, although sparsely decorated. She was looking out the window, when Drake appeared wearing a pair of faded jeans and a dark green cotton shirt. *Don't look, don't look, don't look.* She didn't want to notice how good he looked in casual clothes. He didn't look like a starchy executive dressed like this. He looked like an incredibly attractive, well-built man with gentle hands and lips that could unravel every fiber of her being.

"Would you like to go now or would you like to stay here and relax awhile first?"

"Let's go." She didn't want to relax. She just wanted to get this over with so he would take her home.

While they ate, he asked her about her plans for the weekend.

"I'll be busy Saturday."

"Doing what?"

Kate didn't want to tell him it was her birthday. "I'm going out with Kelsie, Sue, and Missy." She was glad when he didn't press her any farther. He told her about his past weekend of car shopping, smiling as he confessed his last vehicle had been a jeep and he had already planned to get another one before she suggested it. He asked her how she came to have her car and she explained about the uncle she had bought it from years before. It had been the only indulgence she had besides her house. She loved that car.

Later when he drove her back to work so she could pick it up, he grinned, "I wasn't kidding you know. I'll let you drive mine if you'll let me drive your car."

Kate eyed him suspiciously, trying to keep the humor off her face. "You're really just after my car, aren't you? I should warn you, many men have tried, but nobody has succeeded in getting behind the wheel."

Drake's eyes narrowed and lost a bit of their humor. She forced herself not to fidget while he studied her intently, as if he were trying to see deep into the thoughts behind her eyes. Finally he leaned toward her. "Ah, but I don't just want behind the wheel, I want the title too."

Kate shifted uncomfortably in her seat. "Thanks for dinner, I should be getting home now." She opened the door and Drake caught her with a hand on her wrist.

"It's only right since we had our first fight we kiss and make up."

Kate looked around horrified. The last thing she needed was for Drake to kiss her here in the parking lot. "I don't think that's necessary. Especially since I'm not done being mad."

Drake chuckled. "Okay, when are you going to be done being mad?"

"When I'm done you'll be the first to know."

"And how's that?"

Kate looked him right in the eye. "When I'm done being mad at you, I'll take you out to dinner."

A Dream to be Loved

"And kiss me goodnight?"

"Yeah, sure why not," she said, feeling free to agree because she knew it would never happen. She swallowed hard, pushing the sadness she felt at that thought deep inside for now, fearing one day soon all the emotions she'd been forcing down were going to refuse to be buried any longer. Once the dam broke she didn't know if she would survive the flood.

"It's a deal," Drake said. "Would you like me to follow you home to make sure you get there safely?"

He let go of her wrist and she slipped out. "As I've been getting myself to work and back for years, I think I can manage tonight. Thanks anyway."

As she shut the car door, she heard his soft words, "Sweet dreams, Kate."

It was difficult to get to sleep with her mind repeating, *don't dream, don't dream, don't dream.* Between that and contemplating the rumors she would face tomorrow, Kate didn't think she would sleep at all.

Pulling into the parking lot the next morning, she took a deep breath. There was no way to prepare for what she was about to face. She planned to just stay as busy as possible and away from as many people as possible.

Her nerves were shot before she even made it to the cage. She headed right for the back and started checking inventory, hoping to stay out of sight. About the time she started to calm down the bell rang and she nearly jumped out of her skin. She pinched the bridge of her nose and whispered. "Here we go. Just hold your head up and try not to let 'em see you sweat."

By the end of the day, she was in a daze. She went home and flopped on the couch in complete disbelief. Instead of making her life miserable, almost everybody congratulated her and wished her well. She was told endless times how great Drake was and what a nice couple they made. She felt like she had been in the twilight zone all day.

Other than a few guys at lunch joking about her helping them get a pay raise, everybody had treated her like a new bride. Now she was just as uncomfortable, but for a completely different reason. How was she going to get rid of Drake without looking like the bad guy?

She picked up a pillow, placed it over her face, and screamed into it. She had read somewhere that was supposed to be a good way to relieve stress. She just never thought she'd be stressed enough to try it. "What has happened to me?" she yelled.

"We give up. What has happened to you?" Sue asked from the doorway. She strolled in with Missy and Kelsie trailing behind her.

"I need a long vacation." Kate dropped her head back on the cushion. "Somewhere exotic and warm, and where the men don't speak English."

"Sounds great to me," Sue said, "When do we leave?"

"Tomorrow. Think we can get a flight?"

"If you're willing to pay, and be flexible about your final destination, you can always get a flight."

"I'm willing to pay, and as long as it's away from here, I'm not picky about where we go."

"Away from here, or away form him?" Missy asked.

"At this point, it's too often the same thing."

Kelsie stepped in. "So how are things going with Drake?"

"How would I know? You'd have to ask him."

"What does that mean?" Missy looked intrigued.

Kate told them about most of the recent events. Leaving out a few personal details. "I'm looking forward to Saturday. It might even be worth it to put on that getup I bought just to get away with friends for the evening and not have to deal with men." She stretched. "I need some tea, anyone else want some?" They all declined and she went to the kitchen.

*****

The other three looked nervously at each other.

"Maybe we should rethink our plans," said Missy said.

"No" Kelsie surprised the other two. "The plans are made and we'll stick with them. It will work out okay."

"I think so too, but we've never purposely deceived her before, at least not other than just joking around. Do you think she'll be angry?"

"Yes," Sue said, "But eventually when everything works out she'll be glad and get over it. When it comes right down to it though we don't know just how she'll react. So be prepared for anything."

*****

When Saturday came Kate was up early. She had a light breakfast, then went for a walk. It was a cool peaceful morning. The frost that had descended during the night was starting to melt already. She watched squirrels scurrying around and stood quietly as two rabbits in the distance played, running in circles, and kicked their feet in the air. She breathed in the cool crisp air, and for the first time in weeks, felt relaxed and at peace.

Kate walked for about an hour, then slowly returned to the house. Normally her friends came on Saturday mornings, but didn't today since they were all going out that evening. She had told Drake she was busy today so she knew he wouldn't be here either.

After enjoying a leisurely day by herself and a hot bath, she opened the closet and stared at the dress. "Maybe this won't be so bad. Just go with the flow and enjoy yourself."

Draping the dress across the bed, she opened a drawer and removed the required underclothes. Once the teddy was on and she was sliding the silk stockings up her smooth shaven legs, she was impressed at how nice the silk felt against her skin. It took a little time to get the stockings fastened correctly, but once everything was in place she found she wasn't as uncomfortable as she thought she would be. She almost didn't recognize herself when she looked in the mirror. She didn't look nearly as silly as she thought she would. She rarely paid attention to her looks. When she did look in the mirror it was usually just to make sure her clothes were adjusted properly, or she didn't have stains or wrinkles anywhere. Taking a good hard look now, however, she was surprised to find somewhere along the way her body had matured and toned. All the lifting, stretching, and ladder climbing required for her job had tightened and shaped areas she hadn't noticed before.

She slipped into the dress and checked the mirror again. It was a simple design with a fitted bodice, two-inch wide straps that went over her shoulders and a skirt flaring slightly from the hips. It was shorter than she would have liked, but not as short as many she saw women wearing now days. She applied a small amount of mascara and some lip gloss, then added a pair of earrings and a short string of pearls that had been her grandmothers. She brushed her hair thoroughly deciding to leave it down.

She heard the others come in and went to the kitchen to join them. When she walked in, the other three gaped at her. "Wow!" Sue was the first to speak. "Who are you, and what did you do with Kate?"

"You know, this isn't as bad as I thought," replied Kate. "I might not be embarrassed to be seen in public tonight after all."

"Embarrassed," Missy said. "If I looked like you, I would dress like that all the time."

Sue stepped over to her. Before Kate realized what her intentions were she reached out and lifted Kate's skirt. "She actually put it on. Now I'm sure you're an imposter."

Kate shoved her skirt back down. "Give me a break. We all know the birthday rules. This was part of the deal."

"I know, but I still thought you'd try to get out of it somehow."

Kate grinned, "I just decided to pretend to be you for an evening. In the right frame of mind, being trampy could be fun."

Sue looked her up and down. "Much as I hate to admit it, even I don't look that good tonight. I'm glad you haven't always dressed like this. I don't think I would've appreciated the competition." Sue looked her over again. "I suppose it will be alright for tonight though, it is your birthday."

"How gracious of you." Kate grabbed her purse off the counter. "Let's go, I'm hungry."

They all talked and laughed on the forty-five minute ride to the restaurant. It felt good to be out just simply having fun. It seemed like forever since she had done that.

Kelsie had reserved a table and they were seated immediately. It was a small table in a corner by a window over looking the river. The table was partially hidden behind large plants. The restaurant was a quiet elegant place with low lighting and soft music. There was a very cozy feeling to it. Kate was somewhat surprised at how small their table was for the four of them though. They must be booked pretty full tonight. Once they were seated three of them opened menus and Sue opened her purse. She pulled out a lipstick and small mirror. When she was done she held out the lipstick. "Would you like to use this?" she asked Kate. "It would look great on you."

Kate looked at it, "No thank you." Before she could say more Kelsie dropped her napkin and leaned to get it, knocking Kate sideways and into the lipstick. She looked at the red stripe on her shoulder.

"I'm so sorry," Kelsie said.

"It's alright," replied Kate reaching for her own napkin.

"Oh no, don't get lipstick all over the linen napkin. You should go wash it off in the ladies room."

Kate laughed, "What difference does it make? People use these to wipe their mouths all the time. They get lipstick on them then."

Sue stepped in, "Yes, but this stuff doesn't wipe off. You'll have to wash it."

"Okay, where's the ladies room?"

"It's over there," Kelsie answered, "I saw it when we came in."

Kate walked in the direction Kelsie pointed and saw the sign. Sue was right, the lipstick didn't remove easily. It took a few minutes to get it off. She combed her hair and made sure her dress was still covering everything it was supposed to, then went back to the table.

She was almost to the table when something caught her eye. Glancing over she saw a man seated at the bar. He smiled and raised a glass to her. Kate smiled back wondering if he knew her and she simply didn't recognize him in the dim light. She stepped around the plant that hid her table and looked directly into Drake's eyes. She was so stunned she nearly tripped.

Drake stood as she approached, his eyes slowly taking in every inch of her. "You look incredible," he observed in a deep husky tone. Taking her hand he leaned over and kissed her cheek.

Kate just stared at him for a moment too shocked to react, then glanced around. "Where are the others? What are you doing here?" She knew the answers, but her mouth voiced the questions anyway. "I can't believe they did this." Drake pulled her chair out and she sat down. "Was this their idea or yours? Or was it a collaborative effort?"

"We'll discuss who you can be mad at later. Here they left these for you." he pulled three envelopes from the pocket of his jacket. Kate noticed he was very well dressed. The charcoal-gray jacket was tailored well for him. It emphasized his broad shoulders and tapered waist. It also seemed to deepen the color of his eyes.

Kate took the envelopes he handed her and opened the first one as he took his seat. It was a birthday card typical of Sue. Cute and to the point. At the bottom she had written: *I want one just like him for my birthday. Don't do anything I wouldn't do. Love Sue.*

"Like that leaves anything out," mumbled Kate as she shoved it back in the envelope.

"What?"

Kate handed him the card. "It's just Sue trying to be funny." She opened the next one from Missy. This one also had a hand written message at the bottom. *Please don't be too mad, we love you and want you to enjoy your birthday. Love Missy.* She let Drake read it also. The last one, obviously from Kelsie, she opened slowly not sure she wanted to read it. Kelsie was apt to tell her something she didn't want to hear right now. Before completely removing it, she started sliding it back into the envelope.

"Aren't you going to read that one?"

She peeked over the card and saw Drake's inquisitive expression. "Yes, I'll read it." *Remember the drawing*, was all that was written inside this one. Kate stuffed it back into the envelope then tucked it into her purse, blinking back the prickly feeling in her eyes. Drake gave her the other two. She could tell he was curious about the last one, but didn't ask her about it.

Wanting something to hide behind she picked up the menu, perusing it slowly.

"Would you like some champagne to celebrate your birthday?" Drake asked.

She glanced over her menu. "No thank you, I try to stay away from alcohol."

When the server came over, they gave their order. Salads were brought out shortly and she and Drake talked lightly while they ate. The meal was delicious. When all the plates were cleared, Kate was trying to decide if she should have dessert when the server placed a small beautifully decorated cake in front of her. One lone candle stood in the middle, the flame lightly flickering.

Drake took her hand and looked into her eyes. "Make a wish, Kate."

She closed her eyes, not having any idea what to wish for. There was a wish trying to form in the back of her mind, but she refused to give into it. It was beyond the realm of possibility and she was not going to set herself up for that fall. She wasn't going to let herself wish for anything that involved Drake. She couldn't think of a thing. She had already gotten her wish when she moved into her house, and didn't think she had the right to wish for anything else.

Finally, instead of wishing for something more, she decided to be thankful for what she already had. She opened her eyes and blew out the candle.

Drake smiled and served the cake. Then he reached into his jacket pocket and pulled out a small box. It was wrapped in gold paper and tied with a white ribbon. "Happy birthday, Kate." He held it out to her. She hesitated a moment, then carefully took the package.

When the wrapping was off she opened the little white box to find a velvet jewelry case inside. Kate held her breath as she pulled the lid up. Tucked inside was the locket she had told him about one night while they talked in front of the fireplace. She didn't wear much jewelry, but had fallen in love with this locket the first time she saw it. It had been in an antique shop in Pierceton. "I can't believe you remembered," Kate whispered, "I'm surprised it was still there." She blinked back the tears threatening to spill down her cheeks. "You shouldn't have. I know it was expensive, that's why I didn't buy it myself." She tried to steady her voice. "I don't think I can accept it."

"Yes you can, because I won't take it back. I want you to have it. It is very beautiful, it's only fitting that belong to someone as beautiful as you."

Kate blushed. "That's nice of you to say but...."

"Kate." She was trapped by Drake's penetrating stare. "You really are oblivious, aren't you?"

Her brow furrowed. "Gee, thanks."

"I mean you really have no clue as to how beautiful you are, do you?"

Tears tried to form again. "Please don't tease me," she whispered.

He took both her hands in his. "Kate, I'm not teasing, I'm speaking the truth. How can you not truly see something that you look at everyday?"

The server interrupted at that point and asked if they would like anything else. Kate asked for a box for her cake, claiming she was too full to enjoy it. She smiled at the waiter and thanked him for the meal and the cake. He flashed her a smile and told her to come again soon.

When the young man left the table, Drake smiled and shook his head.

"What?" she asked.

"You turn that poor boy to mush with just a smile and accuse me of teasing you when I tell you how beautiful you are." He leaned back in his seat. "I suppose you're going to tell me you didn't notice the man at the bar, either."

She looked confused. "I saw him. I wondered if maybe he recognized me from somewhere. I deal with a lot of salesmen and tool reps from Fort Wayne."

Drake laughed. "What he recognized had nothing to do with tooling." He pushed his chair out. "If you give me your claim check, I'll get our coats."

Kate gave him the small tag out of her purse. She carefully removed the locket from its box while she waited. It was a small silver heart with a single rose engraved in it. Kate loved antiques. She could look at something and dream up entire histories about where they came from and the people who once owned them. As soon as she saw the locket she had pictured a young girl receiving it from her one true love. Family and hard times, however, had kept the two apart and the locket was all she had to feel close to him. She had worn it for many years, until she had finally died of a broken heart having never married. The locket had then been taken and sold in a pawnshop by her spoiled sister who had always been jealous of her. From there it had changed hands many times, being bought and sold by people who couldn't see the love it once held.

Kate giggled. She must be spending too much time around Missy. Her sense of drama was getting out of control. She set the locket in the box and unclasped the pearls she wore. She was about to put them in her purse when the waiter came back with a small stand containing a silver ice bucket with a bottle of champagne in it.

"I'm sorry you must have the wrong table, we didn't order this."

"I know, Miss. It's from the gentleman at the end of the bar. He also said to give you these." He handed her a single red rose and a note. Kate leaned around the plant and peeked toward the bar. The man who had waved at her earlier smiled and held up his glass in a silent toast. Kate straightened in her seat and unfolded the slip of paper she had been given. It read; *Any man who would leave such a beautiful woman sitting alone deserves to lose her. If you ever decide to find a man who will give you the attention you deserve I can be reached at this number. Phillip.*

Chapter Nine

Kate gaped at the note. Surely these had been sent to the wrong table. She was about to look over at the bar again when Drake returned. He sat down draping the coats across his lap. "Did you change your mind about the champagne?" His expression was curious.

"No, I didn't order it."

Noticing the rose and paper in her hand, he asked, "What's that?"

"I think the waiter must be confused and have the wrong table."

He reached out and took the note Kate held toward him. "I think he had the right table." He gave it back to her. "I should thank Phillip for pointing out my mistake. Leaving you alone is not one I'll make again."

Kate picked up her locket and unfastened the clasp.

"Here let me do that for you." Drake set the coats on his chair and stepped behind her. She stood up and pulled her hair out of the way. When he was done he kissed the tiny dimple at the base of her neck, causing a slight shiver to chase down her spine.

After helping her into her coat, he carefully lifted her hair from under the collar. She gathered her things from the table and turned to leave, but Drake stood in her way. He slipped his fingers under the lapels of her coat gently pulling her close and whispered, "This is for Phillip." just before his lips closed over hers.

When he lifted his head her cheeks felt flushed. She wasn't used to such public displays. "Why would you kiss me for Phillip?" She asked slightly flustered.

"So he'll know not to wait by the phone for your call." With a possessive arm at her waist, he guided her from the room.

Drake opened the door when they reached the car but didn't let her immediately get in. Kate gave him a curious look. He smiled. "This is for me." The kiss in the restaurant had been nice, but it didn't compare to this one. His hands slid inside her coat and around her waist, pressing her against him. It was a deep drugging kiss that left her breathless and dizzy.

She was glad for a place to sit when she settled into the car. She lay back against the headrest deciding this was by far the strangest evening she had ever experienced.

They chatted casually on the ride back. Kate relaxed, thinking she would soon be home. As they approached town however he passed the turn to her house. She eyed him suspiciously. "Where are we going?"

"It's still early. I thought we'd stay out a little longer."

A Dream to be Loved

It wasn't long until he pulled into a parking lot. Kate tensed, "I'm not going in there! Not dressed like this, and with you."

"Come on, it'll be fun."

"For you maybe, but not for me."

Drake got out and opened her door. When she didn't attempt to get out, he reached in and scooped her out of the car. She clung to him until her feet were firmly on the ground. She recognized many of the cars in the lot.

"Don't make me go in there. Why are you doing this to me?"

Drake looked into her eyes. "I'm not doing this to you. I'm doing this for you." He kissed her softly. "Sweetheart, somehow you've gotten the wrong impression about yourself. I want to help you see what other people see. You are an incredible woman although you refuse to see it, and you try to keep other people from acknowledging it. Maybe if I can help you see what I do, you'll let me in."

He led her to the door of the all too familiar hangout. Saturday night was a popular night at Pete's and from the look of the cars at least half of the shop was here tonight. Drake held the door and firmly guided her through it. She was standing with her back to the room, facing Drake.

"Can't we do this some other night?"

"No." He slipped her coat off her shoulders and hung it on a hook, followed by his own.

"Hey, Drake!" She heard Steve yell from the pool table. Other familiar voices followed but she was too nervous to turn and look.

"Hi, Drake," this voice wasn't quite as friendly. "Are you going to introduce us?"

"I'm surprised to see you here," came another less than friendly voice. "I thought you were occupied elsewhere these days."

Kate's brows drew together. She wondered why they seemed upset with Drake.

"Yeah, you wouldn't be dealing from a different deck now, would you?" Smitty didn't sound happy at all.

Drake smiled down at her, and with a lowered voice said, "If you don't introduce yourself soon I could end up in the dumpster out back. They've already threatened the life of any man who mistreats their favorite tool crib attendant and they seem to be under the impression I'm cheating on her with you."

It was obvious nobody realized who she was. None of them had ever seen her dressed in anything but jeans and work shirts, or with her hair down.

"They really threatened you?" she asked in disbelief.

"Yes. They didn't know it was me at the time. They were talking about the flower guy, but there was no question about their intentions. Well, there was one question."

"Which was?"

"Whether Smitty got to go first or last."

In a voice soft enough for only Drake to hear, she said. "So if I don't say anything they will beat you to a pulp, and if I do let them see who I am they will think you are a really great guy."

"Right."

Kate narrowed her eyes and tapped her chin looking as if she were weighing her options.

Drake gave an exasperated sigh. Taking her by the shoulders, he spun her around to face the crowd. Kate looked nervously at her coworkers who all gaped at her in turn.

Drake spoke first. "I don't think I really need to introduce her. I'm sure you all know Kate."

Kate felt a deep blush slowly burn across her face as they stared.

"Wow!" After Smitty vocalized that one short word, a chorus of whoops, hollers, and wolf whistles broke out.

Things started to calm down until Steve yelled, "Hey, you never told us you had legs."

"Let me guess," Kate said. "You thought I just floated around on my broom all day."

They all laughed. "What he means," Terry corrected, "Is that you never told us you had legs like that."

Kate looked down. "They're just legs."

Laughter again. "No, those are not 'just legs'. Those are *legs*."

"Let's find a table." Drake placed his hand in the small of her back. They crossed the room and settled in a seat near the pool table.

Steve held out his cue, "Wanna play, Kate?"

When many of the guys gathered around, she realized this dress was not designed for bending over a pool table. It was bad enough so much of her was showing already. They didn't need to see it hiked any higher.

She smiled. "Not tonight, thanks." She stood up and glanced at Drake. "I'm going to get something to drink." Drake followed her to the bar and they both ordered a soda. She took a sip and was going to return to the table when Smitty caught her around the waist and sat her up on the bar. He bent, leaning his forearms on either side of her, so he could look her in the eye.

"If you'd consider dumping the suit," he nodded toward Drake. "I'd consider losing the tattoos."

"Really?" She played along. "That's the best offer I've had all evening."

"She's with me Smitty," Drake said. Not that he looked genuinely worried. Kate had told him about the relationship her and Smitty had.

"Not really," Kate said. "It was either have dinner with him or be stranded in Fort Wayne with no ride home." She glanced in Drake's direction. "Doesn't the fact I have to be tricked and lied to by long time trusted friends before I'll go out with you tell you something?"

Drake leaned on the counter. "Yes. It tells me you're as stubborn as you are beautiful."

She glared at him. "I can find someone else to take me home you know." She cocked an eyebrow. "As a matter of fact I still have Phillip's number. He would probably come and get me."

Drake grinned. "I'm sure he would if you called him, but you no longer have his number."

"Yes I do. It's in my coat pocket."

"No it's not. I took it out when you were distracted in the parking lot." Kate's chin dropped.

"Who's Phillip?" Smitty asked.

She closed her mouth and smiled at him. "He sent me champagne and a rose at the restaurant. There was also a note with his name and phone number on it."

Many eyes turned to Drake. "I went to get our coats and Phillip tried to steal my date."

"Man, that's pretty low. I would never try to steal her behind your back," said Smitty. "I'm not opposed to doing it openly in front of you, though." He turned back to Kate. "So, how 'bout it, darlin'? I'll take you home."

"Sorry, Smitty, I get that privilege." As the other men went back to their activities, Drake excused himself and walked toward the men's room, leaving Kate and Smitty to talk.

Smitty looked at her more serious now. "So what's really going on tonight?"

"It's my birthday." He already knew about the birthday tradition so Kate filled in this year's events for him.

"He's a great guy, Kate. What are you so worried about?"

"Smitty, he's a VP. A suit, as you so eloquently put it."

"You know what that tells me, along with what I've seen of him at work?"

"What?"

"That he's smart and ambitious, and that he has very high standards. He doesn't settle for less than the best. Which is why he likes you. You are definitely the best."

Kate blinked back tears. She hadn't cried in years, and yet it seemed like lately she was doing it every few hours. Enough is enough. Slamming all emotions back down where they belong, she blew air out between pursed lips and grinned at him. "Smitty, there is something I've wanted to do for a very long time. Normally I wouldn't consider actually going through with it, but since there has been nothing normal about tonight, why not?" She lifted her hands and placed them gently at the base of his neck. Slowly she ran them across his massive shoulders and down his biceps, then back up to his neck. She giggled. "Wow. That is just amazing." She gave him a wistful smile. "Oh Smitty, why is it you and I couldn't fall in love and spend the rest of our lives taking care of each other?"

He grinned. "Darlin', I've asked myself that many times over the years. On paper we're perfect for each other. Unfortunately, nature just doesn't seem to see it that way." His eyes roamed over her. "Believe me, I have never regretted it more than I do tonight." He chuckled when she blushed.

"You guys aren't going to think of me differently now you've seen me as a girl, are you?"

Smitty laughed. "I've got news for you, there's not one of us who has ever seen you as anything but one hundred percent pure female. It seemed to make you uncomfortable to have us treat you that way so we haven't. This," he pointed to her dress, "is just icing on the cake."

She looked stunned, and he smiled. "Jeans and work shirts can't hide the kind of woman you are. We've all noticed your figure." He cocked an eyebrow. "Most of us notice it frequently." The fact you don't flaunt it or use it to try to get what you want has gained you respect. We also appreciate you haven't tried to act like a man to fit in. We admire the way you can work so well with us. Not many women would handle it so gracefully."

She was amazed. "I had no idea."

"That's part of your charm, young lady."

She slid her arms around his neck and hugged him. "Thanks, Smitty." Then she whispered, "Promise me we'll always be friends."

He hugged her back, his voice slightly thick as he spoke. "You can always count on me, darlin'. I promise." He straightened and looked her in the eye. "Although I have a feeling I'm not the only one who will be there for you."

She glanced at Drake who had been watching them since returning to the table. "I suppose there's a chance you could be right," she admitted.

Smitty dropped a kiss on her forehead. "Give him a chance. It's obvious he cares about you a lot. Think about it, he knows if he hurts you he'll have to contend with all of us, and he still wants to go out with you. That should tell you something right there."

Kate giggled. "Yes, that he's either genuine, or a complete idiot."

Smitty laughed and lifted her off the bar. "Now go enjoy the rest of your birthday."

For the most part Kate did enjoy the evening. She played darts and beat Drake at a game of shuffleboard. Later after the crowd had thinned, she was on her way to the ladies room when she felt something in her shoe. Sitting down at a corner table she removed the intrusive item and was about to continue on when a paper caught her eye. She recognized it of course. It was a copy of the standard betting pool sheet used in the shop. "What are they betting on now?" she murmured. They constantly had one of these going and it was usually about something silly, just for something to do. When she read the topic of this one though, she was stunned. They had started a bet as to what she had on under her dress. They are betting on my underwear! She glanced around. The few guys that remained were involved in games and not paying any attention to her.

She couldn't help but be somewhat impressed the bet was ten dollars. They rarely went above five. Just as she stood up an uneasy thought hit her. How do they think they're going to find out who won?

On the spur of the moment Kate made a decision. Quickly tucking the paper at her side, she strode to the ladies room. When she returned she carefully dropped it back where she found it making sure no one saw her. Casually strolling over to Drake who was engaged in a dart game at the time, she told him she was getting tired and asked if he would mind taking her home when his game was finished.

"We can leave now if you'd like," he answered.

"No, that's okay, you go ahead and finish your game."

The game finished about fifteen minutes later and they said their good-byes. Kate tried to stay calm but her level of nervousness intensified as they approached her house. Kate was out of the car before Drake had a chance to get out and open her door. She scurried to the house and stopped as she was about to put the key in the lock. Taking a deep breath she repeated *you can do this, you can do this, you can do this.* She unlocked the door and turned to smile at Drake, "Would you like to come in?"

He seemed a bit surprised, "Yes, I would."

Kate led him in. "Would you like something to drink? I should still have some soda, unless my friends finished them off without my knowledge, or I have iced tea, or juice or I could make some lemonade." *Stop babbling, stop babbling, stop babbling.* Take a deep breath and just calm down. She turned to look at him.

"Whatever you have is fine."

"Please, have a seat and I'll get the drinks."

Kate retrieved two sodas from the fridge and set them on the counter. Then she went to a small cupboard in the corner and took out a box wrapped in satiny white paper with delicately embossed roses. She carefully lifted the lid and removed a piece of white chocolate. She had never been able to resist white chocolate. For some reason however, she had yet to touch any of this.

Until now.

She felt like it would somehow be giving in if she ate it. But this was an emergency and called for a dose of chocolate. Unfortunately this was all she had. She took a bite and let it slowly melt on her tongue. She savored the rest of it in small bites as she filled glasses and arranged a plate of snacks. The last bite was melting slowly as she walked into the next room. Drake stood as she entered and offered to take the tray. She jumped when he touched her hand and nearly spilled the drinks. Taking a calming breath as the last of the chocolate dissolved on her tongue, she slid in beside him on the sofa. He gave her another surprised look when she sat so close, but didn't complain.

He took a sip of his soda and set it back on the tray. As he sat back, he draped an arm around her, causing her to tense even more. Knowing if she were going to make this work, she was going to have to relax. She took a deep calming breath and let it out slowly.

With a finger on her chin, Drake gently turned her face to his and looked into her eyes. "What has you so jumpy? I would think by now you'd know I'm not going to attack you. I might kiss you, but I've done that often enough it shouldn't have you so nervous." He leaned forward and kissed her softly. A knowing grin crossed his face as he pulled away. "White chocolate. Something must be wrong if you needed a shot of that. What's going on?"

He's right, I'm not good at games. I'll just come out with it and get it over with. Kate stood up hands on hips and faced him. "Okay, here it is. How exactly do you plan to get me out of this dress?"

Drake looked stunned. "Well, I hadn't planned to get you out of your dress." He stood, giving her an exaggerated leer, wriggling his eyebrows. "But if you'd like me to, I'd be more than happy to oblige."

Kate realized as soon as the words left her mouth she had said it all wrong. She covered her face with a hand and tried to think coherently.

"Ahh..." Drake interrupted her thoughts, "You found out about the bet, didn't you?"

Kate raised her head and replaced the hand on her hip, "Yes I did. I assume you're the one who is supposed to discover the answer. I'd like to know how you thought you were going to find out."

"Well," Drake said. "I hadn't really thought much about it. I didn't find out about the bet until just before we left." He took her hand and pulled her back down onto the sofa. Facing her, he continued, "They did ask me if I would help and I told them I didn't think I could."

"Really?" she whispered.

"Really." He brushed a strand of hair away from her face, and smirked. "Not that I wouldn't be interested in finding out the answer, mind you, but I wouldn't try to get you out of your dress to resolve a bet."

She let out a sigh of relief. "Thank you." She stood up again, paced the floor a few times, then gave him a sheepish grin. "Would you resolve the bet if I asked you to?" The stunned look returned to his face, and she laughed. "I know it sounds strange, but I need you to tell them exactly what is under this dress."

He stood, looking at her suspiciously, "How and why?"

"The how is I'm going to tell you what I'm wearing and you can tell them Monday, at lunch. When they're all together."

"Do you want me to wait until you're there or not?"

"Oh, I definitely want to be there."

Drake cocked his head grinning. "Am I going to be in big trouble with these guys for this?"

"No. You're simply helping them out with a bet. One I don't think they'll be dumb enough to make again. As for the why, I'd like to keep to myself for now if you don't mind."

He looked skeptical, "Why do I feel like those poor guys have been had?"

"Because they have. Will you help me?"

"You're sure you want to do this?"

Her fingers curled into fists at her side and her chin raised a notch. "Yes, I'm sure."

His skepticism was replaced by mischief. He stepped closer and pulled her into his arms. "How will I know if you're telling me the truth about what's under here?" He ran a finger along the edge of the shoulder strap. "I'm not sure I would feel right about going along with this without verifying the answer myself. They'll want to know how I found out. If it was discovered you told me what to say, how would it look? My reputation could be tarnished, I could lose all credibility in the shop and that might jeopardize my job. There's a lot at stake here."

She couldn't contain a grin at the obvious intent behind his statements. Finally, she laughed at the innocent look he was trying to achieve. "As I'm not going to just stand here and drop my dress for you, I guess you'll simply have to take my word for it."

Drake raised an eyebrow in challenge and started running his fingers up and down the length of her back. "I would never expect you to just drop your dress." He leaned forward kissing her cheek. "That would spoil my fun." He increased the pressure of his hands up and down her back as he kissed her. After starting soft and easy he reached up and cupped her face, deepening the kiss. His hands slid down her neck. His fingertips gently massaged across her shoulders, then trailed slow caresses down her arms until he linked his fingers with hers. As his lips left hers, he took a step back and lifted her arms slightly away from her body.

Kate didn't fully understand the satisfied grin on his face until she felt something tickle her foot and looked down. That's when she discovered her dress pooled at her feet. It took a few seconds for conscious thought to force its way through the shock at standing there in nothing but a black teddy and silk stockings.

She felt reality rise in direct proportion to the color flooding her face. She dreaded seeing the humor in Drake's eyes but couldn't stop herself from looking up. What she saw, however, was not smug humor. He was taking in every inch of her teddy and the parts of her that it did and didn't cover. Replacing the humor was a look even someone as inexperienced as Kate could recognize. His eyes returned to hers and held. She wanted to breath but couldn't. His breathing was shallow and strained.

Suddenly he was dragging her back into his arms covering her lips with his. This kiss was long, deep, and urgent, causing her to lose all sense of everything but Drake. Kate was vaguely aware of being lifted and carried to the couch. She felt the weight of his body press her into the cushions. His mouth left hers and started a trail of kisses along her chin and down the side of her neck. "Kate," he whispered against her skin, "you are so beautiful." She heard him draw a ragged breath as he lifted his head. Her eyes opened and locked with his. "If I don't leave now I'm going to tell you, as well as show you, how I feel about you."

Kate didn't immediately release him. She studied him for a moment unsure of what to do. Drake threw his head back and yelled, "Yes!" with a satisfied laugh and hugged her tight. "At least you thought about it and didn't just throw me out. I'm making progress, aren't I?" He kissed her again when she would have spoken, then stood up. "That's good enough for now."

Glancing down the length of her body, he said, "One day soon though, I'm going to tell you. So you'd better get used to the idea." Kate immediately flushed under his gaze and pulled the blanket from the back of the couch, wrapping it around herself.

Drake bent and gave her a slow kiss good-bye. When she opened her eyes again, he whispered, "Happy birthday," then strode over and retrieved his coat. He opened the door and turned, Smiling, he said in that familiar tone, "Sweet dreams, Kate," before disappearing into the night.

Kate sat stupefied, not being able to take everything in. The evening had started out strange and continued to get more bizarre as it progressed. She felt like her whole life had changed in the course of a few hours.

She had come out of childhood into adulthood knowing who she was and how she would spend her life. It would be spent with a good job, working with people she liked, for a company she was proud to work for. It would be lived in a house bought by her no one could take away. She had worked hard and accomplished what she had set out to do and was lucky enough to have gathered close friends along the way.

Not once had a man been part of the master plan. Kate had just accepted at an early age she wouldn't marry. She didn't remember really ever questioning it or being upset about it. She just knew it wouldn't happen.

This man however didn't seem to want to go away. Kate didn't know what to do. She had tried to explain things to him but he wouldn't listen.

Chapter Ten

Monday morning dawned and Kate was glad for the distraction. She was tired of trying to find things to keep her mind off Drake, and trying to convince herself he was not making progress.

After spending the morning focused on work, she felt much better. When the lunch bell ran, Kate headed to the break room. She was about half way through her sandwich when Drake strolled in.

"Hello." He received a round of, "Hi, Drake," in return. Kate stifled a grin as he moseyed over to the pop machine and got a soda. She noticed several of the guys looking at him, then glancing at her. He popped open the can and took a drink, then walked over and stood across the table from her.

He looked around the table. "I believe I have an answer you guys want." Kate noticed some of the men start to fidget. Others made faces and squeezed their eyes shut, as if they could disappear. "Uh, you could tell us later Drake," one of them said.

"Yeah, this might not be the best time," added another.

"I think now is as good a time as any," replied Drake. "It was a black teddy with lace trim and garter."

They all turned to look at Kate. She glared around the table. "Now why would you guys need to know that?"

Steve pulled out his wallet and Terry slowly pulled the crinkled sheet of paper out of his pocket. He scanned the grid and said, "Here it is, someone got it exactly right." He squinted, pulling the paper closer, "The name's so small it's hard to read."

Steve pulled a stack of bills out of his wallet. "Here's the money when you figure out who won."

Terry looked again at the paper, then a look of disbelief eased across his face. He glanced at Kate, then buried his face in the paper again. "I don't believe it," he mumbled.

"Well, who is it?" someone asked.

He turned toward Kate. "It's her."

They all gaped at her for a moment then one of them said, "How did you get your name on there?"

"First of all, you guys should know by now you can't hide things from me." She reached over and picked up the money. Even dared to count it in front of them. "Secondly, you should learn not to leave your grids just lying around on tables unattended." She splayed the money and used it to fan herself. "Well it looks like I'll be eatin' good this week. Thanks, boys." She felt quite smug now, giving her unexpected courage.

A Dream to be Loved

"Well Drake, since you helped make this possible how about a thank you dinner." She waved an arm around the table. "Compliments of the shop."

Drake smiled a slow, unnerving smile. "I would love to have dinner with you, but it would simply be for the enjoyment of your company. Believe me, being shown the teddy was all the thanks I need."

He winked at her and strolled out of the break room as casually as he had entered, leaving her and her crimson glow to face this mob. I'll get him for that, she thought as she picked up her things, head held high, and marched out of the room, pretending not to hear the snickering behind her.

She stopped at the grocery store after work and found Drake waiting in her driveway when she arrived home. He unfolded out of the jeep as she pulled into the garage opening her car door when she shut off the engine. "Hello, I was hoping you'd be home soon. I just got here myself." She climbed out, and rather than shut the door, he slid into the driver's seat. She gave him a cautious look but didn't say anything. "Don't worry I just want to look." He slowly inspected the inside and gave a low whistle. "Nice," was all he said before looking up at her. "I know I'm not allowed to drive it, but do we get to take this when we go to dinner tonight?"

"Sure. But right now you can help me carry the groceries in." She loaded him down with bags and entered the house. They talked about the day as they worked. Kate had noticed the second she saw him he had lost the dress shirt and pleated pants and changed into snug faded jeans and an equally well fitting hunter green pullover. He even had on a pair of tennis shoes. Did he somehow find out how attractive she thought he was dressed like this? And what if he realized she kept handing him all the things that went on the lower shelves of the pantry because it gave her an unobstructed view?

When Drake straightened and turned after the last item was put away, she noticed his brow arch as he looked at her. Not only had he caught her staring, but she wondered just how goofy the grin on her face had been considering her thoughts at the time.

"Is something funny?"

She instantly went as red as she had in the break room this afternoon. "I... uh..." She burst into nervous giggles. "No, not really." His brows drew together. She laughed even harder. She had never behaved this way around a man before. She felt like a twelve-year-old. "Well, um... actually it was funny, but it was one of those you-had-to-be-there things," she stammered.

He didn't look convinced but decided not to question the subject further. "So where are we going tonight?"

"Do you like seafood?" He did so they decided on a small local restaurant that was well known for their fish and shrimp.

Kate enjoyed dinner but decided it was time she made sure Drake didn't read too much into it. She wished she hadn't gotten carried away at lunch and invited him without considering the consequences. She was quiet as she drove home trying to figure out how to convince him this had been a impulsive invitation and he shouldn't take it too seriously. As she pulled into the drive, he turned and smiled at her with his arm resting along the back of her seat. He slid his fingers under her braid and began to caress the back of her neck.

"I enjoyed dinner. Thank you. It's also nice to know you're no longer angry with me."

Kate turned off the engine. "Angry with you?"

Drake laughed. "You said when you were done being mad at me for telling everyone at work about us you'd let me know by asking me to dinner."

After a moment of confusion, the conversation came back to her. She also laughed. "Oh, yeah, I did say that, didn't I? Well, I guess you're off the hook."

"Don't think I've forgotten what else you agreed to."

The look on his face quickly conjured up the second part of the conversation. How could I have forgotten? Her mind scrambled trying to think of a way out of it.

Drake laughed out loud. "Oh no you don't. You agreed and I'm holding you to it."

"Drake, I...."

"You can either kiss me here, or we can get out of the car first. It's up to you, but you have to decide soon because I have some work to catch up on so I can't stay much longer."

"Well, if you're in a hurry it could just wait."

"Oh, I definitely have time for this."

Kate shoved the door open and escaped from the car. Drake also vacated the vehicle and walked around meeting her half way. He took her hand and walked with her to his car. When they reached his door, he dropped her hand and grinned. Making no move toward her.

She glared at him. "You're not going to give me a break here, are you?"

"Nope."

"Drake." She ran a hand through her hair.

His voice lowered. "And I expect a real goodnight kiss. Not some sisterly peck on the cheek."

Kate brought a hand up and covered her eyes, massaging her forehead with her thumb and forefinger. There was no way out of this. She had willingly agreed to it at the time.

She just wished she had remembered before getting into this position. Finally with a sigh of defeat, she lowered her hand. *You can do this, you can do this. You can do this.* She slowly slid her hands up and over

A Dream to be Loved

his shoulders. He still made no attempt to participate. She could tell by the look on his face he was going to leave it all up to her. Stretching up on tiptoe, she let her eyes drift shut as she touched her lips to his.

She felt Drake's arms slip softly around her. She could feel his heartbeat against her own. Knowing if she continued she could get carried away by the sensations rushing through her, she slowly sank back on her heels breaking the kiss.

After a careful breath, she asked, "Was that acceptable?"

Drake smiled, "Yes, that was defiantly acceptable." He dropped his forehead to hers. "As a matter of fact, I would be willing to accept a kiss anytime you wanted to give me one."

Kate squeezed her eyes shut briefly before stepping back. "You have work to do. I'd better let you get home."

He brushed a kiss across her cheek. "Sweet dreams, Kate."

Once in the cage Tuesday morning Kate threw herself into work with a vengeance. After the tooling report, she started pulling all the tools out of the drawers and cleaning the cutting oil and coolant residue out of the slots. When that was done she one by one emptied the polishing supply shelves and scrubbed the dust and grime off them. She was bent with her head stuck between two shelves trying to reach the back when "Hello Kate," reverberated through the enclosed space. Startled, she jerked her head up and smacked it on the metal sheeting above.

Drake grinned when she muttered something very unladylike as she extracted herself from the tiny cave.

Rubbing her head, she glared at him. "What do you want?"

"To see you." He leaned a shoulder against the newly cleaned shelves and crossed his arms over his chest. "I happen to know it's your break time and thought I'd come and see you."

Kate studied him for a long moment, then heaved a long resigned sigh. "You're not going away, are you?"

"Nope."

"Then I think it's time we agreed to some ground rules."

The left side of his mouth curled upward. "We, or me?"

She made an exasperated sound. "Look, I've spent a lot of time thinking the last couple of days." She dropped her rag on a nearby stool, then squared her shoulders as she faced him. Bringing her hands to her hips she continued, "You won't leave me alone, and well, I guess I don't find your company..." she hesitated a moment, cocking her head with a look of concentration obviously choosing her words carefully, "unpleasant. So I suppose there isn't any reason we can't be friends."

Drake groaned, "You aren't giving me the we-can-still-be-friends speech, are you?"

"No, I'm giving you a we-can-only-be-friends speech." She dragged a hand over her hair. "If you agree" another sigh, "I won't object to our spending time together. We could occasionally go out to dinner or a movie or something, but it would just be as friends, not dating," she spat out the last word like it was foul, then glared at him. "If you can't agree to these terms, then you can just go away now."

His stance shifted and his eyes narrowed on her. She stood tense waiting for his answer, and started to fidget. "Drake...."

He held up his hand. "I just needed a minute to think it over. The answer is yes, I'll agree to your terms." He slid his hands into his pockets. "If that's all you can give me, then I'll take what I can get."

She smiled as relief washed over her. "Thanks."

"So does this mean if I was in the mood for pizza tonight, you wouldn't be mad if I asked you to come along?"

"I suppose not."

Drake looked at his watch. "I'd better let you get back to work and I have to go check on a rush job out on the floor." He winked. "See you tonight."

Kate watched him leave then finished wiping down the shelf she had been working on, restocked it, and decided to leave the rest of the shelves for another day. She felt lighter somehow, not so much tense energy needing to be burned off. She felt good about her decision, and Drake's agreement. She could enjoy his company now as she did with other friends without him expecting more from her than she could give.

That evening when Drake showed up she was cleaning up a mess. "I just finished painting a small shelf I want to hang in the kitchen. I need to get cleaned up. Do you mind waiting?"

"Of course not. Take as long as you need."

After a quick shower, she opened her closet and looked around. She pulled out a new pair of jeans and one of the sweaters she had bought and never returned as planned. Not knowing when she would have time to get back to the store, she decided to keep the clothes. It was a pale coral color and soft as down. It was long sleeved and hugged her more tightly than most things she wore. She replaced the antique locket around her neck. It was the perfect accent for the sweater. A nervous flutter caught in her middle when she wondered what Drake would think if he knew, except to shower, she hadn't taken it off since he gave it to her. It wasn't because he had given it to her, it was because she had loved it since the first time she saw it, but was sure Drake would make more out of it. It was the only piece of jewelry she had ever worn to work. She made sure it stayed tucked under her shirt so it didn't get damaged. It was strange, even no longer than she'd had it she felt lost when it wasn't around her neck. She shook herself mentally. "Stop being silly," she mumbled to her reflection. "It's only a necklace."

*****

A Dream to be Loved

Kate was digging through her purse when she entered the kitchen. "I was sure I dropped my keys in her somewhere."

Drake was glad she didn't look at him right away. If he was going to do the friends thing he had to keep his cool, and that sweater did nothing to reduce his temperature. By the time she found her keys, he had regained his composure. Mentioning, "You look nice," in a by-the-way manner as they walked to the car.

"Thanks."

She smiled and he could tell she was much more relaxed now he agreed to her terms. He was pretty sure, in her mind at least, this would keep him at a safe distance. As far as he was concerned, she had just willingly agreed to go out with him. That was a huge step. If she needed this friend not date word game to make her feel more secure about letting him into her life, he would play along. At least for a while. After all, couples should start out good friends.

He glanced her way again, trying not to grin. He knew she didn't dress like that when going out with her female friends. She had dressed up for him, and without being tricked.

He could get into this friends thing. Now that he didn't have to spend the first half of the evening waiting for her to relax, they could get to know each other better faster. He knew she needed to go into this relationship one step at a time and she had finally taken a step toward him. Now was not the time to push her for anything else. He was willing to wait until she was ready for the next step.

*****

Kate had enjoyed the evening. On the ride home however she became curious as to how it would end. Drake had agreed to her just friends rule, would he try to kiss her goodnight? Once parked they both exited the car and Drake walked her to the door.

"Do you want to come in for awhile?"

"I would love to, but I have an early meeting in the morning so I'd better be going." He clapped her shoulder like he would any of his buddies. "Good night. Thanks for the company at dinner," and strolled to his car without a backward glance. He did wave as he pulled out onto the road and drove away.

Kate stared after him, mouth gaping. After several minutes she turned toward the steps stating loudly, "Well it's a good thing he didn't try anything, or he'd have been sorry." She went in the house, curled up on the couch and burst into tears. She didn't want to think about why. She just needed to cry.

Kelsie walked in a short time later. "What's wrong? Why are you crying?"

"Well it's not because of him that's for sure!"

93

"I'll make tea and we can talk."

When she returned with the tea, she listened while Kate explained how glad she was Drake finally understood how she felt and was willing to just be friends.

"Well good," Kelsie said, "I'm sure it's quite a relief not to have a single, gorgeous, successful man chasing after you anymore. That can be so bothersome."

Kate glared at her. "Very funny." She set down her cup and stretched along the back of the couch. "Actually yes, it is a relief. Now I can relax and my life can get back to normal."

Kelsie picked at the fringe on the throw pillow she was holding, and softly asked. "Why are you so afraid to take a chance, Kate?"

Kate looked away. "I've told you he's a VP."

"I didn't buy into that excuse the first time I heard it, and I'm not buying it now. What's the real reason? It's obvious to everyone else Drake doesn't care what you do. It's you he's interested in. I don't believe that's the problem. You don't seem too convinced of it yourself."

Kate burst into tears again. Too many emotions had been bottled up for too long and demanded to be released.

"I don't know why he won't leave me alone. I'm the girl nobody wants. He can't possibly want to be with me. He probably just feels sorry for me now, but he'll get tired of me and leave."

"Why would you think that?"

Kate slid off the couch to retrieve the box of tissues from the small table by the front window. She stood and stared blindly at the fields across the way.

"Nobody has ever wanted me. It's a fact I came to accept a long time ago."

"Kate, I know you were passed around a lot as a kid, but you weren't always unwanted. I remember the year you lived with your cousin and her husband during high school. You really enjoyed that and were the happiest I've ever seen you." Kelsie stood and came up behind her. "I've always thought it was strange you didn't spend more time with them after you moved out."

Kate felt completely defeated. She was drained and didn't have the energy to fight it any longer. "I've never told anyone because it was too humiliating. I couldn't believe I had been so stupid." She removed another tissue from the box wiping her eyes and nose. "You remember how I told you my parents had helped bail my cousin out of a jam when she was younger, and help her get her life back on track?"

"Yes."

"Well, the day I moved out, after I had everything packed and in the car I went back in to say good bye and tell them how much it had meant to me to have stayed there. I was thrilled when I was told they asked if I could live with them. It was the first time I had felt truly wanted anywhere." She caught another tear with her tissue. "I told them how much I appreciated being there, and was about to let them know what it had meant to me, when my cousin hugged me and said it wasn't a problem at all, that she was thrilled to finally have the chance to repay my parents for all they had done for her." Kate couldn't stop the sob that escaped. "I had actually believed they had wanted me, and in the end I had only been a means to repay a debt." She covered her face with the tissue.

Kelsie wrapped her in her arms, hugging her tight. "Kate, I'm so sorry, I had no idea you've been carrying this around with you all these years." She held her until the sobs subsided, then guided her toward the couch easing her into it.

"Kate, none of us get to pick the family we're born into. Nobody knows that better than the four of us. You know that's how we all ended up such close friends." She held Kate away from her and looked into her eyes.

"You may have had problems with your family, but think about this." Kelsie paused a moment to make sure Kate was listening. "Missy, Sue, and I have always wanted you." Kate's head tilted as she took in what her friend said. "We have all been together for a very long time and not once has any of us ever even thought of asking you to move on. As a matter of fact, if you ask any one of us who is the glue that holds us all together we would all say it's you."

It was now Kelsie's turn to cry. "Who do we all call when there is a problem? Who do we run to when we need help, fight with family, need a place to go?" She waved her hand around. "We all come here. We've all had places of our own for quite some time, but this is where we all gather. We all come here. To you."

Kate shook her head, not being able to reconcile what she was hearing with what she had believed for so long. "But...." She didn't know what to say.

"There is no but. Think about what I said. Have you ever once felt unwanted among the three of us? Have you ever once gotten the feeling any of us doesn't want you?"

Kelsie stood, coat in hand, and repeated her request. "Think about what I said. Time has proven there are three people who want you." She wagged her finger at Kate. "Don't think you're getting rid of us any time soon. It's not a far leap to conclude there would be others out there who would want you and love you as well." She slipped her arms into her coat. "I'm going to leave you to think about what I said. Drake is a great guy, who is smart enough to see how great you are."

*****

As the grays and browns of winter gradually morphed into the blues and greens of spring, Drake was true to his word. He treated Kate strictly as a friend. They spent three to five evenings a week together. They occasionally went out with Missy and John, or Kelsie and Tom. He didn't mind when any, or all of the three women, would spend the evening with them at Kate's house. Kate had been to his apartment, but only when he had taken her there she had yet to go on her own. She did however call him occasionally. Most nights they didn't see each other they talked on the phone. Drake felt like he was playing out scenes from When Harry Met Sally.

He was acutely aware however, that although he made sure he kept his distance physically, Kate didn't. Over time she had gradually tried to get closer to him. He noticed her fairly often laying a hand on his arm as they talked. Looping an arm through his as they walked, and sitting against him when they watched TV. He didn't bring this to her attention. He liked that she was warming up to him whether she would admit it or not. But it was getting increasingly difficult not to return those gestures and add a few of his own. He knew she liked having him around. He also knew her feelings for him had grown. What he wasn't sure of was if she was ready to face those feelings yet.

Friday of the first week in May, Drake walked past the cage and saw another employee attending the window. He stopped and asked where Kate was.

"I'm not sure. I was told she had some sort of emergency and won't be in today."

Drake felt his gut wrench. It was the closest to panic he ever remembered being. "Do you know what the emergency is?" he asked, trying not the reach in and shake the information out of her.

"Nope. I was just told to fill in today."

He strode into the office and asked Ray. "I don't know. She called early this morning and said there was some sort of accident and she wouldn't be in. To tell the truth I've been worried about her myself."

Drake forced himself to walk, instead of run, to his office and called Kelsie.

"She called early this morning. Her uncle Max was in an accident. He rolled his pickup truck. I don't know how bad it is or what hospital he's at. When she called she was on her way out the door and didn't give me any details. I'm sorry I should've called you as soon as she hung up, her cell phone was beeping from a low battery when she called. I didn't think about you missing her at work and worrying. It's been a rather hectic morning.

"That's okay," he said, breathing a sigh of relief she wasn't the one hurt. "Do you have any idea how long she'll be gone?"

"No I don't. I'll be sure and call you if I hear from her though."

"Thanks, Kelsie." He hung up the phone, glad she wasn't the one in the accident, but worried she was upset and alone. He tried her cell phone on the slim chance she'd answer, but it went straight to voicemail. He looked at all the work on his desk, knowing he was going to get precious little of it done until he heard from her. Drake spent the rest of the day alternating between checking figures and pacing the floor. After work he went to Kate's house. Sue was there and let him in. They kept each other company for a while before Sue stood saying, "Well I have a date tonight. I was going to cancel and stay here until I knew Kate was okay, but since you're here you can do that." She smiled, "Something tells me you can comfort her better than I can these days."

*****

When Kate dragged through the door around eleven, she was exhausted. The call had come about five that morning and she had left shortly after. By the time she'd driven the two hours to the hospital, they'd moved her uncle to a private room. He had a pretty nasty concussion and a gash on his head but other than that was fine. Her aunt Ruth however was not. It had taken the better part of the day to calm her down. Kate had stayed until her aunt was convinced Max was going to be all right.

She went back to her room and took a hot shower. Donning one of her beloved nightshirts she wandered to the kitchen to make a cup of tea. As tired as she was she knew she wouldn't be able to sleep until she unwound a little so she strolled into the living room, stopping dead in her tracks when she saw Drake through the moonlight asleep on the sofa. She gently placed her cup on the coffee table as her eyes clouded with tears. How many times today had she wanted him to be with her? She couldn't even begin to count. Suddenly all the stress of the day released and she sat crying quietly while watching him sleep. When the tears subsided she gave in to impulse and slowly stood. She crept a step closer and put a hand on either side of him before lowering herself onto him.

His eyes fluttered open as his arms instinctively wrapped around her. She brought a finger to his lips. "I've had a really rough day. I know it would be breaking my own rules, but do you think we could just lie here and kiss awhile?"

His lips formed a slow curve and he carefully rolled, placing her partially against the back of the couch and partially under him, entangling their legs in the process. He slid his hand around hers and drew it away from his mouth. "Oh yeah, we can definitely kiss awhile." He brushed his lips to hers and whispered, "As far as I'm concerned, these lips are yours for as long as you want them."

He kissed her slowly and softly, fulfilling her need for comfort not passion after the day she'd had.

Breathing a soft contented sigh, Kate now felt she was truly home. She hadn't wanted to admit to herself but this house, the house she had worked so hard to get, the house she had waited for and wanted more than anything on earth, hadn't felt like home recently unless Drake was in it. Now, not the house, but here with him, like this, is where home was. She curled her arms around his neck and laced her fingers in his hair. She felt his heart beating with her own. She wanted to be closer to him. Gliding her hands the length of his back, she released his shirt from its confinement of denim and slipped her hands across his back. Her hands took on a mind of their own. Her hands roamed over his exposed skin, her fingers tracing every muscle.

They were both breathless and lost in what they were doing when a shrill ring startled them. The answering machine picked up and Sue's voice seemed to echo through the room. "Hi it's Sue. I was just checking to see if you were home yet. Catch ya later."

When all was quiet again, Drake started trailing kisses down the side of her neck. Suddenly, Kate burst into giggles. He raised his head and looked at her his brow arched. She laughed again. "I'm sorry, I'm not laughing at you. It's just... I never did this as a teenager. It suddenly struck me how glad I am we don't have to worry about one of our parents walking in and catching us.

Drake grinned. "I'm glad, too." He dipped down and kissed her again.

Kate hugged him tight, then released a slow groan. "We may not have to worry about parents, but I haven't called Missy, Sue, or Kelsie since I got back. One of them could walk in at any time looking for me."

Drake dropped his forehead to her shoulder with a moan. Kate laughed, "I'd better call them." Drake pushed himself up and looked down the length of her body. Blushing instantly, Kate straightened her shirt.

Reluctantly, he dragged himself off the couch. She sat up and they heard a noise from the kitchen. Sure enough, someone had come to make sure she was all right.

Kate quickly refastened a few buttons open on her shirt as Drake straightened his. He flipped on the light just before Kelsie walked in the room. She looked from one to the other taking in their appearance. Fighting a grin, she said, "Am I interrupting something?"

Drake grinned back, tucking his shirt it. "No. We were just, ah... talking."

"I see," Kelsie replied.

He looked at Kate and held out his hand. She took it and allowed him to pull her off the sofa. "Why don't you walk me to the door. I'll go and let you two have some time to talk."

Kate stepped outside with him. Taking her in his arms, he pressed his lips to hers. "I'd better warn you now. After tonight, I can't go back to that platonic just friends relationship."

"Drake--"

He placed a finger over her mouth. "I mean it, Kate. I can't, and won't, go back to that. And if you were honest, I don't think you want to either."

After kissing her one last time, he whispered, "Sweet dreams, Kate," against her cheek, then made his way through the darkness. Yet again tears rolled down her face. It was the first time in months she had heard him say that and was amazed at how good it felt to hear it.

Chapter Eleven

The next morning all four of Kate's closest friends were milling around her kitchen. Sue was making coffee, Kelsie was pulling baked goods out of a bag, Missy was setting the table and Drake was cooking eggs and pancakes. He loaded a tray with an assortment of food and two glasses of juice a few minutes later.

Sue looked at the tray and smiled. "She's always cranky when she first wakes up."

"I'll try to remember that. Anything else about her I should know?"

"Yes, but you've probably already figured out most of it by now. Like the fact she's terribly stubborn."

"How about the way she eats those little snack cakes. Peeling them apart layer by layer instead of just biting into them," Missy said.

Kelsie joined in, "She squeezes the toothpaste from the middle instead of the end, and she just rolls the bread wrapper under instead of putting the twist tie back on it."

Drake chuckled then asked, "Is she less cranky after something to eat?"

"Most of the time," Sue answered, "But I'm not guaranteeing anything."

"I'll take my chances. If I'm not out in three or four hours come and save me, okay?" He wriggled his eyebrows and turned toward the hall.

"Sure thing." They laughed as he left the room.

Balancing the tray, he walked down the hall and carefully opened her door. Kate was asleep with a sheet draped lightly across her hips and legs.

Drake set the tray down on the nightstand. Easing himself onto the bed, he slowly lifted the partially unbuttoned nightshirt away from her midsection.

*****

"Mmmmm..." Kate's brows creased as the haze of sleep slowly faded and she realized that deeply erotic sound had just escaped from her. She felt the most incredible sensations chasing themselves around her body. She heard a soft chuckle and carefully opened her eyes. Drake was softly caressing the skin of her abdomen with his fingers and lips. A shiver shot up her spine, and goose bumps broke out all over her body. Drake gave another low husky laugh.

"Good morning."

A Dream to be Loved

"Good morning." She blushed at the soft breathless draw of her voice.

Drake made his way up from her belly button to the underside of her chin. Kate's lips parted and let a soft whimper escaped.

After a brief good morning kiss, Drake released her lips. He drew in a ragged breath and groaned, "You'd better get up." He pulled her left hand out of his hair and brought it to his lips. "I don't want to finish this until I know it's a permanent situation." He then deliberately kissed the base of her ring finger and felt her body tense. "Are you ready to admit how you feel about me yet? Or let me tell you how I feel?"

She was trapped in those eyes. She felt like he could see clear to her core and it still scared her. She had always kept that part of herself so tightly guarded she didn't think she would ever be able to open it to anyone. She finally had to Kelsie, but she didn't think she could to Drake, and he deserved someone who was willing to give herself completely and freely to him. He deserved someone better than her. Tears began to stream down her face.

Drake gently brushed the tears away. He heaved a deep sigh. "Kate, am I off base here? I'm convinced you care about me. You know I have feelings for you, and I'm pretty sure you know how deeply they run. What I don't understand is what's holding you back." He leaned up on one elbow, running a hand through his hair. "Am I wrong about how you feel? Have I totally misjudged the situation?"

Kate slid out of bed. She looked at him; her eyes still damp. "Drake, I..." She paced back and forth across the rug, wringing her hands. "I just am not sure I can do this."

She stepped into the bathroom and shut the door.

*****

Drake flopped back on the bed in frustration. Had he misjudged things? He figured given time she would get over whatever fear she had. He had been patient while spending months simply being her friend, letting her get comfortable with him. He knew she cared about him. He knew she was attracted to him physically. So what was it? Maybe she really just didn't love him.

He stood up and wandered around, looking at pictures and knick-knacks scattered about the room. He noticed a sketchpad on a chair by the door. He picked it up and started leafing through it, amazed at the drawings inside. He recognized different views of the landscape around her house. Various animals and places around town took up other pages. Momentarily distracted, he asked, "Kate, did you draw all these." As he turned another page, the bathroom door burst open.

He started to look up but the image on the page he had just uncovered caught his attention. His face stared back at him. It was such an incredible likeness; there was no need for the name that was scrolled across the corner. He found something unnerving about the eyes, as if his soul was somehow exposed on that page. Then another thought hit him.

*****

Kate could tell as soon as she opened to door she was too late. The look on his face told her he had found it. She stood riveted while she waited for his response.

He stared at the sketch. A multitude of expressions chasing around his face. Finally, after what seemed like an eternity, his eyes lifted and again trapped hers. "You do love me," was all he said. She wanted to speak. Wanted to deny it, scream, cry, something but she couldn't move. They simply stood there, each staring at the other.

There was a light knock on the door, then Sue coughed in an obvious manner. "Excuse me, I hate to interrupt anything that might be going on in there, but Drake has a phone call."

"Come in," said Kate, her voice was barely a squeak, but she was impressed she got any sound out at all.

Sue opened the door, breaking the spell the two were in. She held out the phone and said, "Sorry, Drake, it started ringing in your coat pocket. I hope you don't mind I answered it. It's Bill Denison."

He took the phone automatically. "No, I don't mind, thanks."

Kate stepped over and sat on the bed, convinced her legs wouldn't hold her much longer.

From the one end of the conversation she heard, and the look on Drake's face, Kate could tell it wasn't good news. When he hung up, he walked over and sat beside her.

He put a hand over hers. "That was Bill. Our plant in England had a titanium fire that got out of control and damaged part of the shop and some of the machines. He wants me to go assess the damage personally."

Kate tried to swallow the lump developing in her throat. Trying to find her normal voice, she asked, "When do you leave?"

"This afternoon if possible. He told me he would call me back with the travel arrangements." He took her in his arms. "I'll probably be gone at least a week."

I will not cry, I will not cry, I will not cry. Kate realized she hadn't gone a full week without seeing him since meeting him. She cleared her throat and pulled away from him standing up. *Pull yourself together.* She shook herself mentally and turned to look at him. "Is there anything you need done while you're gone? Plants watered, fish fed, mail brought in?"

He smiled and took her hand pulling her onto his lap. "If you don't mind you could pick up the mail and paper. I don't have any fish or plants."

A Dream to be Loved

"No plants? I thought everybody had plants." She was glad he wasn't pushing her about the sketch.

"Well, I don't. I just haven't gotten around to getting any. And besides it wouldn't do me any good. I was definitely not born with a green thumb. I would just end up killing them." He reached in his pocket and took out his key ring. He removed two keys and handed them to her. "This one is to my apartment, and this one is for the mailbox."

"If you give these to me now, how are you going to get in to pack?"

"I'll have the landlady let me in." He wriggled his eyebrows, "She likes me."

"I'll just bet she does," mumbled Kate. Irritated to find herself disliking a woman she had never met.

Drake, obviously pleased with her reaction, squeezed her tight. "Yes, she does. And I like her too. We've become very close."

"Then maybe she should get your mail. Since she already has a key and lives in the same building. How handy for her." She grated, getting increasingly angry with herself for her response.

"It really would help me out if you could do that for me."

"Can do. Anything else you need?"

He leered at her suggestively and she laughed. "I don't think so. Even if I were so inclined, you have to go home and pack."

He heaved a dramatic sigh. "Okay. I do have to pack. I hope I have enough time to say goodbye to the landlady." She tried not to react, but couldn't stop the glare she gave him. With a mischievous self satisfied grin, he kissed her goodbye and told her he would let her know what his travel arrangements were as soon as he knew.

*****

The final bell rang and Kate was relieved. She couldn't believe how slow work was going this week. It just wasn't the same knowing Drake wasn't in the building. Instead of going home, she drove to Drake's apartment as she had done for the past two days. She stepped in the main door and retrieved his mail. She secured the box and wandered toward the elevator. While she was waiting, a noise echoed down the hall. A petite elderly lady maneuvered a walker toward her.

The woman broke into a smile. "You must be Kate."

Kate's brows drew together. "Yes, I am. How did you know?"

"Drake described you perfectly. I would've known you anywhere." When she was close enough, she held out her hand. "I'm Lila Miller. I'm the landlady here. Actually, my son owns the building and when my husband passed away I moved in here. I collect the rent. I'm not capable of doing much more these days."

Kate felt herself flush slightly, feeling foolish as she shook the other lady's hand. "Nice to meet you." She was definitely not the trashy little tramp trying to get her hooks into Drake, Kate had imagined.

"Oh, it's nice to finally meet you too. Drake has told me so much about you. He indulges me by sitting and talking with me when he comes home from work. He knows I don't get much company." She got a look of mischief about her. "He even brings me pistachio ice cream from the shop in town since I can't get there on my own anymore. He knows it's my favorite."

The elevator door opened, "Would you like to come up with me?" Kate offered. "I was just going to take his mail and paper up. We could chat on the way."

Lila beamed. "If you're sure you don't mind."

"I don't mind at all." Kate held the door while the older lady scooted in. It was obvious this woman was lonely. Kate's heart went out to her. She liked Lila instantly and understood why Drake did too. She could just throttle him, however, for giving her the wrong impression. On the other hand, she had to blink back tears at the thought of him making a special trip to the ice cream stand to bring his widowed landlady her favorite ice cream.

After spending almost an hour getting to know Lila, Kate went home, deciding not to return the next day without pistachio ice cream.

*****

Early Saturday morning, Kate stopped at a local garden center to buy a plant. Drake had called her a couple of times from Europe to update her on his progress and she knew he would be home late that evening.

Spending the past week without him had given her time to think. For a long time she tried to put what Kelsie said out of her mind, but it would creep in at times when she was with Drake. Possibilities would waft around the outskirts of her mind, not really fully formed, but like shadows drifting in and out of the evening light.

She was still afraid to let herself believe he would truly want her, and yet, he was still around. Still called regularly, still came over often, still came by at work to talk to her. He showed no signs of being ready to be rid of her even after all this time. Even though it frightened her, she was becoming increasingly aware she didn't want to live without him. She had herself almost convinced maybe he did really love her. Maybe he did really want to spend his life with her. Maybe he wasn't just using her as a distraction until someone better came along. Maybe there really was something about her someone could love. After all, like Kelsie said, she still had her friends and they still wanted her. Maybe she wouldn't have to spend the rest of her life alone.

A Dream to be Loved

As she hiked the large potted plant into the elevator, she smiled. She would leave the plant and tell him she would be willing to help him keep it alive if he wanted. Wondering if she had the courage to actually say the 'L' word out loud, she stepped off the elevator and unlocked the door.

The plant slipped, and in the process of trying to catch it, she knocked the door open.

Inside stood a woman in a peach silk robe. Dark brown hair floated around her shoulders. Startled, the woman squealed, bringing a slim hand with long bright red nails up to her face.

Drake came into the room, wearing only a pair of jeans and drying his hair with a bath towel.

"What's all the commotion?"

Stunned, Kate dropped the plant and ran for the stairs. Drake pulled the towel from his face just in time to see her turn and leave.

Kate got in her car and just drove. She cried so hard she didn't know how she managed to stay on the road. She had been so afraid this would happen. That someday she would convince herself someone could love her, then have the rug yanked out from under her. She had managed to avoid this type of pain her entire adult life. She had accepted how things were years ago, how could she be so stupid? Again?

Hours later, she ended up at her cousin Cheryl's house. Her face swollen and red. She didn't tell Cheryl the whole story and knew she wouldn't ask. Kate just needed a place to stay where Drake couldn't find her. After spending the rest of that day and all of the next taking long walks and crying, Kate knew it was time to go home.

It was almost one in the morning when she pulled into her drive. Kelsie's car was sitting in front of the house; she was relieved it wasn't Drake's. She dragged herself out of the car. As she entered the house, Kelsie met her at the door. "It's about time you got here. Where have you been? We've all been worried sick."

"I've been at Cheryl's."

"Drake left about an hour ago. I convinced him he should go get some sleep. He was going to camp here until you returned, but he has to be at work tomorrow to update them on the situation in Europe."

Kate breathed a sigh of relief. At least she wouldn't have to face him tonight. She'd call in and take tomorrow off. Even if Drake wasn't going to be there she was in no shape to work. At this point she still didn't know what she was going to do about her job. She just didn't think she could continue working there knowing she would have to face him day after day. There were other orthopedic companies in town. She had enough experience, she could probably find another job fairly quickly.

Kelsie smiled at her. "You really are a mess, aren't you?"

"Thanks for noticing." Kate said, dropping onto the couch.

"Are you ready to put yourself out of this misery yet and tell him you love him?"

Kate glared at her, too tired for any more tears. "It's a little late for that now."

Kelsie's voice softened. "Do you really think Drake's the type of guy who would spend so much time with you while sleeping with another woman?"

A tear slipped down Kate's cheek. "I didn't think he was but...." she didn't finish, just shrugged a shoulder.

Kelsie rested a hand on Kate's arm and slowly explained. "Kate, the woman you saw in Drake's apartment was his sister."

Kate's head slowly lifted and she looked at her friend. "His sister?"

"Yes, his sister. He called his parents from Europe and discovered she was going to be flying into the same airport the same day he was, only much earlier. He was able to book an earlier flight to meet her. He told his family about you and they're all eager to meet you. Drake and his sister rented a car in Detroit and drove here because it was going to be quicker than waiting on the next flight to Fort Wayne. They were tired when they got back so after a short rest they were getting cleaned up to come and see you when you walked in, Kelsie said. "I've met Wendy, she's really nice and feels terrible about the misunderstanding. You startled her, then ran away before she could explain who she was. She had to leave this afternoon."

Kate dropped her head in her hands. "I'm such an idiot." She burst into tears, surprised she had any left. "Do you think he'll forgive me for being so stupid?"

Kelsie laughed, "I don't think that'll be a problem." She patted Kate's shoulder. "Why don't you go get some sleep. I'll call the others and let them know you're okay."

"Thanks." Kate didn't have the energy to get up. She just kicked her shoes off and fell sideways on the sofa.

Before Kelsie left, she said, "I don't know if Drake will be able to call you anytime soon. He said he had meetings all day tomorrow. Anything else he could put off, but the damage was pretty extensive over there and needs immediate attention."

"I understand. Maybe that's good. It will give me more time to figure out how to apologize for making such a huge mistake."

*****

The next morning, Drake was frantic. He had been so tired he slept through his alarm and was now running half an hour late. He tried to call Kate during the drive to work, but she didn't answer. He did manage to reach Kelsie. He at least knew Kate was home and she knew about his sister, but he wouldn't feel completely relieved until he talked to her himself.

By three-thirty, Drake was at his wits' end. He had been hustled from one conference room to another all day, having to recite facts, figures, and projections when all he wanted to do was talk to Kate. Having been told she called in for a vacation day, he was back to being frantic. He tried to call her during his short lunch break, but again there was no answer.

He looked at his watch again, only five minutes since the last time he checked. He tapped the crystal, wondering if the battery was getting low and it was losing time.

Bill noticed the gesture. "I think we could all use a break. Why don't we all stretch our legs a little?"

Drake stood immediately. He left the room so quickly he almost knocked down the lobby receptionist. "I'm sorry, Cindy. Wow, that's quite a load you have there."

She grinned, "Yes, it is, Mr. Hampton. And it's for you."

He stood dumbstruck staring at her. "Me?"

"Yes. Here you go." She handed him a large vase with what looked to be two dozen roses and a small white box with a silver ribbon.

"I... thanks." he stammered. Bill was the only one left in the conference room. Drake stepped in and set the flowers down. Opening the small white box, he saw a note on top tissue paper. He unfolded it and read, *This is to apologize for being such an idiot. Hopefully, this will tell you how sorry I truly am. Kate*

Drake pulled back the tissue and grinned. The box was full of white chocolate. He set it down and removed the larger than standard card from the flowers. When he pulled it from the envelope a small object wrapped in tissue paper fell out. He caught it and read the card. *I'm hoping you can find it in your heart to forgive me for all that I've put you trough. On the chance that you haven't given up on me completely, I wanted to make sure you had a way to find me so I can finally tell you how I feel about you. She knows the way home, Kate.*

He slowly unwrapped the small object to find a well-worn key with a mustang emblem on it. He threw his head back and yelled, "Yes!"

Bill jumped slightly, then laughed. "Good news?"

"Bill, I know these meetings are important, but you're going to have to do the last one without me. Right now there's a much more important proposal I need to take care of."

Bill slapped him on the shoulder. "Congratulations! You go right ahead. I'll finish up here. Tell Kate I'm happy for you both."

"Thanks, Bill."

*****

Kate had been pacing the floor for the last hour. Looking at the clock with every pass. Had he gotten them yet? Would he come over? Would he listen to her if he did? Had he given up on her? The questions were endless, and about to drive Kate insane.

Finally, she heard her car come up the drive. Her whole body began to tremble.

Drake didn't bother to knock. He pushed open the front door. She stood with her arms wrapped tight around her middle. They simply stared for a moment, each unable to breathe.

"Kate..."

Tears clouded her eye. She slowly walked to him. "Drake, I'm sorry," she whispered.

"Kate, there's nothing to be sorry for."

She reached out and took his hand leading him to the sofa. When he was seated, she sat on the coffee table facing him still holding his hand.

"Kate--"

She shook her head and held up her hand to quiet him. "Drake, I know I've put you through an awful lot, and you deserve an explanation."

She looked down at their entwined fingers and started to speak. "I was passed around from family member to family member most of my childhood. I know those people loved me, but the way someone loves any member of an extended family. I was never special enough for any one person to want to keep me. I was taken in when someone felt obligated, or wanted to do my parents a favor. But no one ever just wanted me for me. The people I've been closest to are Sue, Missy, and Kelsie. We were all misfits in school, and with our families, so we stuck together." She smiled slightly, "They've always teased me about my obsession of owning my own house."

She drew a shaky breath, "I've always needed that stability. I needed to have a place that was mine. A place where other people could come and go if they needed, but that I could stay forever. A house where no one could tell me I have to move because they need my room for someone else. A place where I can feel safe and not wonder who's going to replace me, and when. A home where everyone that comes through the door is equally important."

"I came to accept early on when my friends were all talking about someday getting married and having children, that those things would never be an option for me. That no one would ever love me enough to want me around all the time. I've been very careful to not let myself become attracted to a man so I wouldn't have to deal with the heartbreak when they found someone more important."

Tears were now streaming down her face. She chanced her first look at Drake. She looked back down, knowing if she watched him she wouldn't be able to continue.

"I've loved this house from the first moment I saw it. I knew it was a place I could feel at home. Feel safe. Secure in the fact it was mine."

She looked back at Drake. "Until recently that is. Lately, I haven't felt safe. I've felt so vulnerable. You came in and ripped the security out from under me. I tried to tell you to go away, but you wouldn't. I tried to explain to you I couldn't handle a serious relationship, but you didn't listen. You wouldn't simply turn away like everybody else had. I realized some time ago how deep my feelings for you had grown, but I figured I would eventually get over it and my life would get back to normal. But you didn't get tired of me and leave." Her head dipped as she ran a hand across her cheek to wipe the tears.

"I also realized not long ago this house no longer felt like home. Being with you did. I only felt that sense of peace when you were around. I started to let myself believe maybe you really would stick around. Maybe you really did care enough about me to stay. I let myself think it might be okay if I allowed myself to have a relationship with you. It seems silly now, but I bought you a plant and was going to let you know I wanted to be around enough to help you keep it alive. I was even contemplating telling you how I felt that day."

She drew in a breath and blew it slowly between her lips. "Then I walked into your apartment and, well, obviously mistook the situation. What I couldn't mistake though, is what I felt when I thought you had turned to someone else. I knew right then these were not feelings I would ever get over." Her eyes came up and locked with his. "I love you, Drake."

He dragged her into his arms, squeezing her so tight she could barely breathe. She wasn't sure which one of them was trembling more.

"Kate, I have loved you since the day I met you. I can assure you that you have been, are, and always will be the most important person in my life." He sat her back on the coffee table and reached into his pocket. He slid off the couch and dropped to one knee. Kate, still trembling, brought a hand to her mouth. He took her left hand. "I've wanted to ask you this for so long. Kate, will you marry me?"

Sure she wouldn't be able to push words through her vocal cords, she nodded her acceptance. Drake slid the most beautiful diamond ring Kate had ever seen onto her finger and pulled her into his arms, with tears welling up in both their eyes as he kissed her.

Sliding her onto his lap, Drake held her tight until her breathing was normal and she stopped trembling. "We need to discuss eventual living arrangements." He turned her face to his and grinned. "I've not looked for a house myself because I was waiting until we could decide together where we wanted to live."

Astonished, she said, "Pretty sure of yourself, aren't you?"

His eyes sparkled. "Just optimistic." He tucked a stray lock of hair behind her ear. "I know how much this house means to you. I want you to know, I wouldn't ask you to move."

She dropped a soft kiss on his cheek. "I appreciate that, I really do, but I think it would be best if we found a house together." She sat up so she could see him better. "This house helped me probably more than anyone could know. It gave me the security and stability I needed, and a sense of belonging." She looked around and sighed. "I love this house, and always will, but I don't belong here anymore." Emotions threatened to engulf her, but she managed to get the words out. "I don't belong alone, in my house, anymore. I think we belong together, in our house, wherever that may be."

*****

Now emotions threatened to engulf him. Because of the lump in his throat, instead of speaking, he pulled her close showing her with a kiss how much that meant to him.

The phone rang startling them, but neither moved to answer it. Sue left a quick message and hung up.

Drake dropped his forehead to hers. "You know I like your friends, and don't mind having them around, but do you think we could do something about this open door policy of yours? At least for a little while?"

Kate laughed, wrapping her arms around his shoulders. "They all have keys. How about a call-before-you-come policy?"

"Great. Now, however, I think you should call them so they can congratulate you on your wonderful new fiancé."

Kate threw her head back with a laugh, "My wonderfully modest new fiancé," she corrected, feeling happier than she ever remembered being.

The End

About Kandi Jaynes

Born and raised in Northern Indiana, I live on a quiet country road with my husband, two lovely daughters, and our many animals. I try to enjoy all aspects of life from work to relaxation, traveling and exploring new places, to simply curling up in my yard swing with a good book. I'm a firm believer in the phrase laughter is the best medicine, and believe nothing is as bad as it seems if you can find some measure of humor in it.

Made in the USA
Middletown, DE
20 April 2016